The Carnation House

by Josie Kuhn

Wandering in the Words Press

Requests for permission should be sent to Wandering in the Words Press:
2131 Burns St, Nashville, Tennessee, 37216
www.wanderinginthewordspress.com

Published by
WANDERING IN THE WORDS PRESS

ISBN-10: 099107873X
ISBN-13: 978-0-9910787-3-8

First Edition

For Liz

TABLE OF CONTENTS

CHAPTER ONE
Marvin's Meatloaf

It's Bingo night at the nursing home—the closest thing I will get to a Saturday night date.

My name is Jessica Lee James, born and raised in Celina, Tennessee, named by my father after my great aunt Jessica on my mother's side. My mother didn't figure out my name would be Jessie James 'til after I was born and Daddy started calling me his "Little Outlaw." She never forgave him and never called me Jessie in her life, always Jessica Lee.

My parents passed away a year ago. Only four weeks apart. My mom died of a stroke and my dad a broken heart.

I am a musician, 39 years of age. Today is my birthday, the big four–oh.

I've always said, "Life can change in the blink of an eye." One minute I was singing along to the radio. The next, I was being cut out of my not-so Grand Am with the "jaws of life."

I have been a bed-ridden patient at the state-owned, Carnation House in Nashville, Tennessee, for six weeks, in a room with two other women, one of whom soils her sheets three times a day. The orderlies change them once a day. I think someone must be sneaking her Krystal burgers. The stench is mind blowing.

The other woman seems content with her morphine drip and remote. The TV remains on 24/7. Today, I am getting a wheelchair, and tonight, I will go to Bingo. It is all I can think about.

Nurse Kelly dances into the room with her auburn curls, green eyes and beaming smile. She pushes a shiny silver wheelchair with a big, red bow on it.

"Okay, Jessie," she says. "I have your birthday present."

The nurses have been slowly acclimating me to sitting up. This was hell at first, but now I can sit up for 30 minutes—enough for two hands of Bingo. I am more than ready. I fling myself up and over into the wheelchair like an Olympic pole-vaulter. The chair feels like a throne. All of a sudden I have power, freedom, wings.

"Well" Kelly asks, "How does it feel?"

"Perfect! Thank you!" I say, already

steering out the door. Roomie number one has just let go of another bag of Krystals.

I get to the hall. *Right? Left?* I head towards the patients lounge. This is my first taste of freedom in months, and it is sweeter than molasses on hot-buttered biscuits.

The lounge is a big square room, furnished with a few tables and chairs, a well-worn sofa, a recliner, pool table and a 24-inch TV. It's tuned to a CNN broadcast that no one is watching.

The biggest black man I have ever seen is sitting in a wheelchair at a table. In front of him is a half-finished jigsaw puzzle. He is not big as in *fat* but as in *big*. He has a shaved head and wears a gold hoop earring and a pair of sunglasses.

Kelly has followed me into the room.

"Jessie, let me introduce you to your fellow patients."

"You mean inmates," says the large black man.

"Everyone," Kelly continues. "This is Jessie, and this is her first day in her wheelchair."

A beautiful young girl, about 20, jumps off the sofa. Her waist-length hair is the color of newly mown hay. Her eyes are bluer than a Montana sky. She is wearing a pink terrycloth robe and pink poodle head slippers.

"Hi Jessie! I'm Sissy!" Coincidentally, she

looks like a dead ringer for Sissy Spacek in the movie *Carrie*. She extends a delicate hand for a shake.

"This here is Ray," she says, looking at the humongous man.

"But we call him Ray-Ban because he always, always has his Ray-Bans on."

The black man glances up at me for a second. "Hey," he says. His voice sounds like gravel on a hot dusty road. Immediately he returns his gaze to his puzzle.

"And this is Margaret, but she likes to be called Maggie," Sissy continues, looking at a stooped old woman bent over a *Seventeen* magazine. "Maggie used to be a famous model, didn't you, Maggie?"

Maggie looks up from her magazine. She is pale, rail thin and wears a platinum blonde wig of curls on her head. Her face is a well-worn highway map.

"Well! I beg your pardon," the old woman says. She looks up from the magazine. "Used to be? I will have you know that I am still very much in demand. Why, just yesterday I had a call from my agent. They want me to do a cover shoot for *Vogue*."

I look at Sissy quizzically.

"She's got the old-timers disease," she whispers in my ear.

"It's called Alzheimer's, Sissy," says an elderly man sitting in the recliner.

He rises and extends his hand to me.

"This is Mr. Jones," Sissy says, "but we call him The Professor. This is Jessie."

Mr. Jones, aka The Professor, looks like something out of a Dickens' novel. He has a shock of white hair and a mustache and beard of the same color. He wears a tweed jacket, complete with elbow patches, even though it is the middle of August. In his pocket sits a corncob pipe, and he wears an ascot around his neck.

"Ah, Jesse. A pleasure to make your acquaintance," he says.

I think I have slipped through a time warp and that he might kiss my hand. But to my relief he just gives it a soft shake.

"You don't perchance play chess, my dear, do you?" His eyes widen with hope.

"No. I'm a musician," I say.

How stupid. Like musicians never play chess.

"But I'm sure I can learn," I add.

Maybe it wasn't so stupid. I have never known a musician who played chess.

"Splendid, splendid!" he says, returning to his chair. "Musician? Classical?"

"No. Rock."

"Oh," he says, looking a bit deflated.

Suddenly a high-pitched wail starts down the hall followed by a string of cuss words.

"Fuck! Fuck! Fuck!"

"What the hell is that?" I ask, almost jumping out of my wheelchair.

" Oh that's just Toenail," Sissy explains.

"Tonell, Sissy." corrects Kelly.

"Right, To*nell*... But we call him Toenail."

"Mr. Tonell has Tourette's," Kelly adds.

"What the hell is that?" I ask.

Ray-Ban glances up at me. "He can't help but keep cursing."

"Why?" I ask.

Kelly shrugs. "It's just the way the disease manifests itself. I'll go check on him." She leaves. The "fucks" turn into "shits" and other profanities I don't even want to repeat. No one seems to be paying any attention to the cursing, except for Sissy. She stands grimacing and holding her ears.

A thin, ebony-skinned woman enters the lounge, pushing a cart filled with pitchers and cups. Her kinky black hair is tied into two braids with long yellow ribbons. Around her neck she wears more ribbons, cascading down her chest like strings of pearls. Around her scrubs is yet another yellow ribbon tied around her waist. She looks like a Christmas present ready to be opened.

"Okay, y'all. I got some cold refreshments for y'all."

"Do you have any coffee perchance, Shanika?" asks Mr. Jones.

"*Cold* refreshments, Mr. Jones. "Y'all know where the coffee pot is."

"But there's never any coffee in it!"

"Well then, make y'alls own. Don't take

no rocket scientist man to make a pot a coffee."

"Do you have any pop?" Sissy asks.

"No, jus' lemonade 'n' tea."

"Is the tea sweetened?" asks Maggie, looking up from her magazine.

"No, Maggie, y'all have to fix it y'alls' self."

"Well, do you have Splenda?"

"Miss Maggie, now you knows we only gots sugar an' Sweet'N Low."

"I like Splenda," huffs Maggie. "It melts easier. Sweet'N Low makes the tea taste funny, and sugar doesn't melt unless you put it in when the tea is still warm. If you put it in later, it makes the tea cloudy and ends up in the bottom of the pitcher and—"

Shanika rolls her eyes. "Do you want some or not, Miss Maggie?"

"I'll just have a lemonade," Maggie answers. "You do know that you have to add the sugar to the lemonade while it's still warm, don't you?"

"It's from a carton."

"Oh, all right. I'll have the lemonade. I just hope they got it right at the lemonade plant."

Shanika pours the rest of us drinks and starts to leave. "Y'all wear me out, ah swear, but praise Jesus. Here come Mr. Marvin with y'alls' supper." She wheels her cart out as a big fat man comes in. He looks like a sumo wrestler.

"Hey kids. I took the liberty to bring your lunch in here," Marvin says, carrying five trays stacked on top of each other like they were pieces of notepaper.

"Ooh, smells good, Marvin," says Sissy. "Whatcha got us?"

"I made y'all a blackened catfish, fried okra and a sweet potato pie," he answers.

Ray-Ban looks up from his puzzle. "Blackened? As in burnt?"

"No, Ray. Blackened as in Cajun style."

"I never heard of anyone burnin' a perfectly good catfish on purpose," Ray-Ban says. "S'posed to fry it in cornmeal."

"Why don't you give it a try, Ray?" Marvin nearly slams the tray down in front of him. "You just may like it."

I open up the silver lid. The smell makes my mouth water. "Oh Marvin, this looks great!"

This is the first meal I've had in months. They've been giving me nothing but soup, Jell-O, and Boost.

"Are you Cajun, Marvin?" I ask, my mouth half full.

"No, I am actually Creole, with a bit of Cherokee."

"I'm part Creek and Choctaw," I say between bites. "Also some Rumanian and Welsh."

"Well eat up, Pocahontas, 'for it gets cold.

"Oh, Marvin, this is so good," I say.

"I'm glad you like it." He smiles, but then looks down at the floor.

"Something bothering you, Marvin?" asks The Professor.

"Well, might as well tell y'all… I got some bad news."

We all look at him expectantly.

"Tonight will be my last meal here. I got laid off."

"What?" we all say.

"Why?" Sissy asks.

Marvin shrugs his sumo shoulders. "Got something to do with the state cutting back expenses, all's I know. Bubba's gonna be cookin' for you from now on."

"Bubba!" Sissy says. She looks like she is about to cry. "He can't even boil an egg. He always burns the toast. We'll all die of malnutrition."

"Sorry, kids," says Marvin, looking like he is about to cry, too. "But I'm makin' y'all my meatloaf tonight… My last meal here."

Sissy flings herself off the sofa and into Marvin's bulk. She comes up to about his waist, and her arms reach only a quarter of the way around it. "Oh, Marvin, we will all miss you so much!"

I look over at Ray-Ban. He is shoveling huge bites of catfish into his mouth.

"How is it, Ray?" asks Marvin with a

chuckle.

"Best thing I ever ate."

Marvin smiles and guides Sissy back to the sofa.

"Well, eat up while it's still hot," he says. "Y'all be good to one another, hear?"

We finish our meals in silence, except for Sissy, who whimpers like a hurt puppy.

After the lunch, I am tired and everything hurts. Sissy wheels me back to the room and reminds me—about three times—that tonight is Bingo. I get back into bed and lie down. I am asleep as soon as I hit the pillow.

***

I am onstage in Holland, playing to a nice listening audience. I am in the middle of a song when I break a string. I replace it. And as soon as I start the song again, another one breaks. Then another. The audience members start to get up and leave, one by one, until finally, I am all alone in the concert hall. Then it starts to rain. Harder and harder.

***

I wake up to the sound of rain falling outside my window. It is storming. Thunder. Loud enough to muffle the sound of the damn TV and my two snoring roomies.

I lie there and stare at the cracks in the

ceiling, which I have counted so many times before. The tears start slowly and then erupt into full-fledged sobs.

"Jessie?"

Kelly stands over me with a concerned look on her face. "Are you okay, sweetie?"

"Oh, Kelly, I really fucked up my life! I'll never play music again!"

"Jessie, don't say that. Of course, you will."

"Yeah, right. How many musicians you know play in a wheelchair? It's hard enough getting gigs at 40, never mind being disabled."

Kelly sits down on my bed and tenderly strokes my arm. "Jessie, there have been countless musicians who have been handicapped."

"Yeah? Name one."

She thinks a minute. "Well, Ray Charles."

"That's *one*."

"And, what's his name... Ronnie Milsap! And besides, you are not always going to be in the wheelchair. You're going to start physical therapy next week. You wouldn't be in here if they didn't think you were going to improve."

She strokes the hair out of my face. "Now, cheer up. Tonight's Bingo."

She makes it sound like it's Christmas Eve.

"I hear they have some pretty good prizes

tonight."

"Yeah, like what?" I ask. "Stool softeners and a personalized bedpan?"

Kelly laughs and jabs me softly on the arm. "Come on. Sit up. I'll brush your hair a bit."

I sit up, and she brushes my hair.

"You married, Kelly?" I ask.

"Yes, I am. Ten years now to a wonderful man, Jimmy. He cooks like a gourmet chef, helps me clean, takes care of the kids during the day *and* works a 12-hour night shift. I couldn't do it without him."

"What's he do?"

"He's a fireman," she says.

"Tell me about your kids," I continue.

"Well, there's Danny, who is 8, Tommy, who is 6, and Susie who is 3 going on 16. Here, wait, I have a picture."

She pulls out a cellphone from her pocket, and shows it to me. The perfect family photo. All five of them, redheaded and freckle-faced, with the biggest grins I have ever seen. In the foreground, sits a beautiful collie, also with a big grin on his face.

"What's your dog's name?"

"That's Cheyenne. We also have two cats, Miss Kitty and Mouse."

"Mouse? You have a cat named Mouse?"

Kelly laughs. "When he was a kitten, Miss Kitty used to chase him around, and he would hide in the cupboards and then pop out when she wasn't looking and eat her food like a little mouse. Hence the name."

"Cute." I laugh, thinking of how perfect her life is. Not jealous. Not even envious. Happy for her. She seems so happy and is always so kind to everyone.

Kelly hands me a mirror. "See how pretty you look with just a little fixin' up."

"I haven't looked in a mirror for months," I say.

"For heaven's sake. Why not?"

"Because I don't want to see how disfigured I am. I broke every bone in my face in the accident."

"Disfigured? You're not disfigured at all, sweetie… Here, look."

She tries to make me look into the mirror but I turn my head away.

"Jessie," she continues. "The plastic surgeon you had did a great job. He put implants in your jaw and in your cheekbones. You have Faye Dunaway cheekbones."

I have been told I am pretty, in an exotic kind of way, maybe due to my Native American ancestry. My eyes are kind of slanted upward, my nose a bit too long, my cheekbones too high, and my lips, especially my upper one, too full.

She thrusts the mirror in front of me. "See? Not so bad at all!"

"Kelly, my hair!" My hair, which used to

be a rich sable brown, is now a dull reddish color. "Why is it so red?"

"Probably from all the meds, sweetie. Nothing a bit of Miss Clairol can't fix."

I look again. The somewhat upward slanted eyes are mine, even though I've been told one eye was hanging out of its socket. I can't tell about my nose, because it has a bandage covering it. The mouth is definitely not mine. My full upper lip is gone, replaced by a Reba upper lip.

"Where's my lip?" I ask.

"You can get some Juvéderm when you get out of here, give you Jolie lips. Then you will have Faye's cheeks and Jolie's lips."

She smiles and takes the mirror from me. "Dinner should be here soon. Marvin's meatloaf. And then, Bingo. Gotta go finish my rounds."

Shanika whirls into the room, ribbons flying.

"Aw right, ladies… Dinner is served."

She sets my tray down on my bedside table and delivers the others to my roomies. I open the silver lid. The smell is intoxicating, and I start to salivate immediately. Marvin's meatloaf. Real mashed potatoes with gravy, and lima beans. There is also a small salad with mandarin orange slices, a chocolate brownie with whipped cream and the ever-present factory-made lemonade.

I dig in. It tastes as good as it smells.

"So?" asks Shanika, hands on hips.

"It's incredible," I answer, the words sounding like, "increbel," since my mouth is stuffed full. "Marvin is a top-notch chef."

Shanika smiles smugly as if she had cooked it herself and walks out.

Morphine Drip and Krystal Burger do not even budge from their sleep, their trays untouched.

The thought of stealing their meatloaf crosses my mind more than once.

I finish every last bite, and lie back, smiling. A damn good birthday all in all: a wheelchair, Bingo, and Marvin's meatloaf. *Who could ask for more?*

CHAPTER TWO
Bingo

I awake with a start to the loudspeaker.

"Ladies and gentlemen... Just 15 minutes 'til Bingo!" Please make your way to the patients lounge. It's Bingo time!"

Oh my God! I throw on my robe and slipper—I only need one—and fling myself onto my throne. My right foot is swathed in a sea of bandages, metal bars, and a big black boot. The doctor who saved my foot was a miracle worker. He performed five surgeries and put in plates and rods. He is one under God in my book. If not for his perseverance, dedication and kindness, I would be an amputee.

I take my time heading to the lounge, actually brushing my hair a bit before I wheel out of the room. When was the last time it was washed besides with that God-awful dry shit? I used to love taking long baths, "Lebowski baths," I called them. Bubbles, scented candles, a glass of merlot, new age music. The simplest of joys gone forever. I sigh and head down the long, narrow hallway.

The nurses station is buzzing. Patients mill about. I wheel on through, unnoticed. I glance into the rooms as I go by. In one room there is an old black woman sleeping. Another room is curtained off. The next room is empty.

Empty? Maybe I could get that room. No more TV or Krystals.

I make a mental note to ask about it as soon as Bingo is over.

The lounge is packed. Sissy, Ray-Ban, and The Professor sit at a table together. The rest of the tables are full.

"Jessie! Over here. We saved you a spot!" Sissy calls.

She's dressed up for the night. Her hair is pulled back and tied with pink ribbons. A pink ribbon hangs from her neck… *Maybe Shanika dressed her up.*

I wheel over to the table.

"Thanks, guys," I say.

"No problem, Jessie. Here's your card."

I look at the card. Some of my lucky numbers are on it: 4, 14, 17 and 22. At that moment, a large black woman struts into the room. I have seen her a few times. Her name is Layla, but she is really a man. A transvestite. She wears powder blue scrubs with kitten heels. Her hair is the color of a ripe pumpkin and her makeup is flawless.

Sissy jumps up. "Layla! Your hair!"

Layla touches her locks. "Do you like it? It came out more orange than the picture on the box. It's called henna and it's all natural."

"Yes. I love it! You look like Halloween!"

Layla heads for a desk in front of the room that has been set up with the Bingo machine. "Okay. Everybody ready?"

The room is abuzz with excitement. Everyone looks at his or her card as if it is a gold bar.

"Okay, first number, G-47. G-47, everyone."

"Bingo!" shouts Maggie.

"Maggie, you know the game," says The Professor. You have to get all five numbers in a row, not just one."

"Oh that's right. Silly me."

"Okay, next number is I-22. I-22."

I mark it on my card. The game continues on for a few more minutes, Layla's deep baritone calling out the numbers.

"All I need is a B-9," Ray-Ban mutters.

"I need a B-9, also," says Maggie with a smirk. "It's been three days."

Sissy and I look over at each other and start to crack up.

"Maybe you should get you some Milk of Magnesia," Sissy cackles.

Suddenly Mr. Toenail, who has been seated at a table, quiet 'til now, yells out. "B-

9! B-9! Shit, shit, shit!"

The room explodes in laughter. Layla lets everyone calm down a bit before continuing, although she can hardly contain herself either.

"Okay, okay. Enough already. What, are we in second grade?" she scolds.

"Hopefully Ray-Ban is in the second-grade toilet stall," someone yells.

"Number two, is that next?" yells another comedian.

"Don't listen to that crap, Ray-Ban," yells someone else.

"Crap, crap, crap!" yells Toenail.

"Hey. Let's call Ray-Ban, Ray-Ban the Rooster. Ca-ca doodie do!"

And so on and so on.

Layla looks exasperated. "Okay, come on gang... Settle down. Next number is..." She looks at the number and starts laughing. "B-9!"

"Bingo!" yells Ray-Ban over the laughter in the room. "Ha! Now see who gets the last laugh!"

Everyone gets serious again and the games go on.

Sissy wins one, so does Maggie and then I win on lucky number 14.

"Okay, come on, Jessie, let's go see what prizes they have!" Sissy says, pushing my chair helter skelter to the prize table. The table is loaded with everything from candy to soap, to drugstore perfume and books. Patients push and shove as if it were Black Friday.

"Oh look!" yells Sissy, pointing to a stuffed pink poodle that matches her slippers. Before she can grab it, a tall, big boned, angry-faced woman takes the poodle.

"No!" Sissy cries. "That's mine!"

"You know the rules, girlie," snarls the woman. "First one who touches the prize gets the prize."

"Oh no! I wanted that poodle so bad!" Sissy sobs. Long wet tears flood her face.

I wheel over to mean redneck mama. "Excuse me," I say.

The woman turns and gives me a hard look. "What do *you* want?"

"I'd like that poodle, please," I say, a look on my face as hard as hers.

"Oh yeah? And what are you gonna git me for it?"

I don't have any money on me but I do have my wedding ring. My husband and I divorced a year ago, after a two-year bittersweet marriage. Mostly bitter. He hasn't been to see me once since the accident, even though he lives about three miles away from the nursing home. I look at the band on my finger. It means nothing to me.

"It's gold," I say, slipping it off and handing it to her. She looks at it, then reaches for it and examines it closely. She tries it on her ring finger, but it's too small. She puts it on her pinkie and holds it out in front of her, admiring it. Then she thrusts the poodle at me, smirks and walks away. I wheel back to Sissy, who is still sobbing, and hand her the poodle.

"You got him!" I watch as her eyes turn from gray back to the Montana sky.

"Oh, Jessie, thank you!" She leans over and hugs me so hard I think she may break another rib.

"What are you going to pick, Jessie?"

I look over at the table. There are only a few things left. The candy is gone. Only a few bars of hotel soap and a pair of state-issued socks remain.

"What about this?" asks Sissy handing me a Zoloft-branded pen. "You could start writing songs again!"

"Perfect," I say, although I doubt I will have any inspiration for a song in the near future.

"Well, that sure was fun," says Sissy, hugging her poodle to her heart.

Ray-Ban starts to wheel past us. "Ray, look what Jessie got me!" She holds the poodle in front of him for inspection.

"Very nice, Sissy," he says. "Matches your slippers."

"I know! What did you get?" she asks.

"I got me a calendar so I can write down all my important dates and events coming up," he says.

"Oh what a good idea," Sissy says, oblivious to the sarcasm. "Well, see you later." She looks at me. "I'll wheel you back to your room if you want. Here, you hold him. I'm gonna name him Jessie after you," she smiles and then looks confused. "Jessie is one of those names that can be a girl or boy's name, right?"

"Right." I say, wondering how she has determined it is a boy poodle. She hands me "Jessie" for safekeeping and wheels me back to my room. A lone tear falls down my face as I think of how important the little things are in life and how just one little act of kindness can make such a difference.

CHAPTER THREE
Smoke Break

Darkness falls over the nursing home like Dracula's cape. The joking is over.

Steely eyed Nurse Ratcheds replace Kelly, Shanika and Layla. It feels like an institution for the criminally insane. Cold, dark and mean.

And tonight there is another storm raging outside. The thunder is constant, and lightning bolts shoot thru the sky, making the nursing home seem even more like an evil sanitarium.

I lie in my bed trying to read but I am lonesome and I hurt. I look at the clock. My medications are a half hour late. I buzz the nurses station. No one answers. I buzz again. No one.

"Yes?" someone finally snarls.

"Hi. It's Jessie in room 20. I need my meds."

"Hold your horses. They're coming."

I lie back against my pillow. I have been on 600 milligrams of morphine or MS Contin a day for two months. Enough to kill a horse or an elephant or both. One blue pill every eight hours. It doesn't get me high, or groggy, just dulls the constant pain in every bone in my body.

Twenty minutes later, a tall gaunt woman in her 50s, someone whom I have never seen before, walks in with the medication trays. She delivers the meds to my roomies and then comes to me.

"Here," she says thrusting the small paper cup at me. I take the cup but it is empty.

"There's nothing in here!" I say.

"What do you mean? You just took it!" she says, starting to walk out of the room.

"I didn't take it! You gave me an empty cup!"

"Don't talk back to me. I saw you take it. Now stop your whining and leave me alone." She storms out.

I stare down at the cup. *Did I take it?* No. I didn't. I *know* I didn't. I look around and see there isn't even a glass of water around. I would have needed a sip to wash down the pill.

Am I losing my mind?

***

I wake to the oh-so-sweet sounds of nurses' carts squealing through the halls.

Patients' voices call out. Toenail yells good morning in his own special way. For some reason it all sounds like home. Safe, secure, a million miles away from the confusion of last night.

"Meds, ladies."

It is Kelly looking quite beautiful in her pale green scrubs. Like an angel almost. I swear I can see a golden halo above her head. Her long auburn curls, tied with a green ribbon, cascade down her back.

Another Shanika makeover? Maybe a new fashion statement. A contagious trend.

"Hi Kelly." I try to smile. "I need to talk to you." I take the little cup from her. Inside is the MS Contin.

Kelly pours me a glass of water and hands it to me.

I take the pill into my mouth and swallow. Then I look up at her. "Kelly, I didn't get my meds last night."

"What do you mean? Why not?"

I tell her about the mean nurse trying to give me an empty cup.

"Are you *sure* you didn't take it? Maybe you were tired and don't remember. Remember, it was the first night you have been out of this room in quite some time. Maybe it was all the excitement."

"Kelly. I'm sure. I looked around and there wasn't even a glass of water nearby."

She frowns.

Kelly listens intently, her brows furrowing. "Jessie, maybe you dreamt it. If it happens again, we'll do something about it. Okay?"

"Okay."

She pats my arm. "Shanika is on her way in with breakfast."

Morphine Drip is actually awake and sitting up looking at the TV. I have never seen her sitting up. I look at her. She is pretty in a hard-life kind of way. But her eyes. Her eyes are cold. And then she looks at me. Hard. And makes a face. Like a feral cat. Her lips curl back. I swear I hear her hiss. I look away quickly.

***

"Breakfast y'all." Shanika dances into the room wearing yellow polka dot scrubs. Yellow ribbons everywhere. She presents the trays to my roomies and then sets mine down in front of me. No silver lid on the food today.

Mmmm. A Boost drink, a cup of watered down Tang, and a cup of coffee the color of diluted tea. On the plate there is one soggy piece of bacon, one slimy undercooked egg and Bubba's famous burnt toast. I opt for the Boost and wonder how long one could survive on it alone. *A week? A month?*

Shanika looks at me as if reading my

thoughts. "Looks pretty yucky if you ask me," she says. "Sho' ain't Marvin's French toast with strawberries."

Marvin. I never got to taste his breakfast. My mouth waters as I think of French toast. Shanika looks at me. "Got some strawberry yogurt in the fridge. You wan' some? Look like you can't be eatin' this shit."

"I would *love* some strawberry yogurt. Thank you."

"Ah be raht back then." She takes my tray and waltzes out the door.

"I woulda eat that," yells roomie number two.

Maybe it isn't the Krystal burgers after all.

I sit back and pick up my book. Then I see the Zoloft pen on my table. Beside it is a school notebook I have never seen before. I pick it up. It contains a few doodles and stick drawings on the first few pages but the rest is blank paper. On the inside cover is an inscription.

> *To Jessie. Thank you for Jessie the poodle! I figured you mite need some paper to go with that pen so you can right your songs. Or maybe even a BOOK!!!!!*
> *Luv,*
> *Sissy*
>
> *Oh P.S. Sorry some of the paper was used up.*

I feel like I have known Sissy my whole life. *Why is she here?* She doesn't appear sick. Maybe a bit childish. She is smart. And caring. And funny. I vow to ask Kelly about her.

I want to be out of the room. I get myself into the wheelchair just as Shanika comes in with my yogurt.

"Here ya are. Goin' for smoke break?"

Smoke break? I never knew they *had* smoke breaks here.

"No. Just to the lounge. Thanks for the yogurt."

"No problem." She whirls out of the room.

***

The lounge is packed. Why all the people?

Ray-Ban is at his usual place in front of his jigsaw puzzle. I wheel over to him.

"Hey Ray." I look down at his puzzle. It's a castle. Almost done except for the turrets. I point out a piece to him, but he glares at me and covers the puzzle with his huge arms, as if he were protecting his last meal.

"Back off. I do the puzzles by myself. Don't need no help."

"Okay. Okay. Sorry."

I wonder what Ray-Ban would do if he came in and found someone at his table with the puzzle completed. The image makes me chuckle.

"Jessie!" Sissy is seated at her regular place on the sofa next to Maggie. The Professor's chair is empty. I smile at Sissy. She is so beautiful, so sweet in her pinkness.

Does she ever wear a different color?

"Are you going for smoke break?" she asks.

"I quit smoking after the accident." Well I didn't really quit. I was forced to. Kinda hard to smoke with a trach embedded in your throat. Suddenly the idea of a cigarette seems wonderful. Better than a lobster dinner on a Mexican beach.

"Yeah, I don't smoke either," Sissy says. "But I go anyway. Otherwise it feels like I'm missing out on an adventure."

The Professor walks in. I have never seen him walk before. He's always in his chair. He walks with a limp and a cane.

"Ladies, Gents, Ray, good morning." He walks over to Ray-Ban and hands him a dollar and then shuffles to his recliner.

"Oh yeah, here's mine and Maggie's," says Sissy. She gets up and hands him two one-dollar bills. She turns to me. "The four of us chip in for the lottery everyday."

Ray-Ban looks up. "You want in?"

"Sure, why not? But I don't have any money on me. Have to get it from my room."

"Don't worry. I'll cover you today. Give me two tomorrow."

"Cool. Thanks."

"Ray-Ban sneaks out during smoke break and walks down to the gas station at the end of the block," Sissy explains.

Walks?

"Shhhhh." Ray-Ban puts his huge black index finger in front of his mouth. It is as long as my hand. Maybe my foot.

"Attention everyone," a voice comes over the loudspeaker. "Smoke break in ten. If you want to smoke, please make your way to the lounge. Thank you."

That's why there are so many people in the lounge. It isn't just for a happy, social breakfast.

"God, I wish I had a cigarette," I say.

Ray-Ban gets out a pack of KOOLs.

He hands me two of them. "I'll put it on your tab."

"You're the best, Ray. Where do we go to smoke?"

"Out that door. On the porch."

"Cool. Thanks." I wheel towards the door.

"But you can't go yet, Jessie!" Sissy says. "You have to wait for the nurse to open the door."

"I can open it myself," I say.

"No you can't. The nurse is the only one who knows the secret combination."

"Secret combination? What is this, *I Spy?*"

Finally, a voice comes blaring over the loud speaker like the ringmaster at Barnum and Baileys. "Ladies and gentlemen, and children of all ages over 18, it is now time for your 9:15 smoke break. Please make your way to the designated smoking areas immediately."

The Professor gets his corncob pipe out of his tweed jacket and starts to fill it. Maggie puts down her magazine and pulls a gold cigarette case out of a pocket in her robe. She takes out what looks like a Virginia Slim.

Layla struts in the room, her orange hair done up on top her head. She really does look like a pumpkin. "Y'all ready?"

The patients start lining up. Some even push and shove to get outside first.

"Come on!" Sissy wheels me to the door.

The smoking area is a long covered porch with some chairs and benches scattered about. It overlooks a grassy area that edges up to the woods. It is actually quite pretty. I think I can hear a small creek in the distance.

There are not enough seats for all the patients, and they scramble for a spot like in that old musical chairs game. Ray-Ban wheels over to the very end of the porch. Sissy wheels me after him. Maggie and The Professor follow. I see that the porch wraps around the building and leads to a few stairs.

"This is *our* spot." Sissy plops herself

down on the steps.

Maggie and The Professor lean against the railing. The Professor glances back around the corner before lighting his pipe.

"It's pretty." I take out one of Ray-Ban's smokes. The Professor pulls out an old silver lighter and lights me up and then does the same for Maggie and Ray-Ban.

I take a puff and start choking. It has been almost two months since I have smoked. This is a *KOOL*. No filter. Ray-Ban glances at The Professor who looks down the porch and then gives Ray-Ban a nod. Ray-Ban gets up out of his wheelchair and walks perfectly down the stairs and disappears around the corner.

"I didn't know he could walk," I say.

"Neither does the staff," The Professor says.

"Why is he in here then?"

"Maybe beats the hell outta being homeless," The Professor says.

"So, Jessie," says Sissy. "Have you heard about all the stuff with the state?"

"The state?"

"Yeah. They're talkin' about shutting this place down."

"Why?" I ask.

"Too many problems," she says.

"Like what?"

Sissy looks at me. "Problems like the nurses using terms of adornment with the patients."

"Terms of endearment?"

"Oh yeah. Endearment," she says. "Like 'sweetie.' Or 'honey.'"

"And 'dear.'" adds Maggie.

"But this is the South," I say. "Terms of endearment are an everyday occurrence. It's just the way we talk. It's normal."

The Professor takes a long drag on his pipe. "Not enough money. There are also problems with the patients and the staff fooling around. I even heard a rumor about patients not getting their meds and drugs being smuggled out."

I almost choke.

Maybe I didn't get my pill, after all.

I look at him, but he is looking out at the wooded area.

"This property is worth about two mil," says The Professor. "They can't close it to sell it without a list of complaints."

"But what about the patients?" I ask. "Where will we go?"

"They'll split us all up into different nursing homes."

"But I like it here," Sissy says. "Y'all are like my family. You *are* my family."

"So when's all this supposed to happen?" I ask.

The Professor shrugs. "I heard talk of some state people maybe coming sometime this week to check the place out."

"Oh man," I say. "What a bummer."

Suddenly Ray-Ban comes up the stairs and gets back into his wheel chair. "Wooly Bully!" he yells.

I look at him and follow his gaze to the woods.

"Wooly Bully, come on boy."

A big mangy tiger stripe cat comes slinking out of the woods. He sits down on the grass and looks over at us.

"Wooly Boy, come on. Gotch'u some of Marvin's meatloaf from last night!"

The big cat yawns and makes his way across the grassy area. He comes right up the steps, and brushes his mangy legs against Ray-Ban's.

Ray-Ban reaches down and pets the ugly cat with his huge hands.

Ray-Ban, *the gentle giant.*

He looks at the cat almost lovingly. The cat jumps onto his lap. Ray-Ban takes a napkin out of his pocket. The cat licks up the meatloaf right in Ray-Ban's lap.

"Good ain't it boy?"

I look at him with my mouth wide open.

"Hi, Wooly," says Sissy. She scratches the cat's ears.

Wooly finishes the treat and lies down on Ray's lap, purring.

"He's wild?'"

"Yeah," Ray-Ban says. "There's another one around here, too. A black one. The patients call her Miss Pearl, but she don't come anywhere close."

I take out the other cigarette, and The Professor is right there with his lighter for me. We all—except for Sissy—smoke in silence, petting Wooly Bully and looking out at the woods.

I stare at the trees and think about how nice it would be to run off into those woods and be free. Be out of here, out of the wheelchair, out of the craziness. To spend the day catching mice. And snuggling up with Miss Pearl. Wooly and Miss P.

Layla's voice coming from the far end of the porch breaks the reverie.

"Okay, gang. That's it. Let's go. Smoke break is over."

The patients start to file back, not in so much of a hurry this time.

"Sorry boy." Ray-Ban gingerly lifts the cat off his lap and sets him down on the porch. "See ya later."

Wooly looks up, meows once like he's also saying, "See ya later," and disappears down the stairs and back into the woods.

I don't want to leave. I look at Sissy. She looks like she doesn't want to leave either. Without a word she gets behind my chair and wheels me towards the door and into the lounge. Most of the patients shuffle back to their rooms, except for us five. *The family. As Sissy calls us.* She wheels me over to our table and then returns to her spot on the sofa where Maggie is already deep into her magazine. The same *Seventeen* magazine she was reading yesterday.

Yesterday? Has it been only one day?

Ray-Ban wheels over and looks down at his puzzle. I look at the remaining pieces and can see where each one goes. But I hold my tongue. I glance over at Sissy. She has a very faraway look in her eyes. She doesn't look right. She looks like she is in a trance.

Suddenly she jumps off the sofa, frantic. "Get them off of me!" She swats at her arms and legs. "Ye-ow! Get them *off!*"

"Sissy! What?" I wheel over to her.

"The spiders! They're all over me! Get them *off!*" She rakes her fingers furiously through her hair. Long blonde strands fall to the floor.

"Sissy, there are no spiders." I try to grab her arms but she is too strong. "Sissy!"

"They're making a web around me!"

Layla rushes in and gets a bear hug grip on her. Sissy goes limp.

Kelly rushes in, and together they get Sissy on the couch.

"There, there." Kelly says, patting Sissy's arm. "No more spiders, sweetie." She brushes Sissy's hair back from her face.

Sissy looks around the room. "What happened?"

"Just a little episode, honey," Kelly says.

"You're all right now. Here take this." Kelly hands her a pill and a glass of water.

Sissy obediently takes it.

"Fuck. Shit. Piss!" Toenail screams from down the hall.

"Oh my Lord!" Kelly says. "When it rains it pours!"

"I'll see to him." Layla rushes out the door.

"Come on, Sissy," says Kelly. "Let's go back to your room. I'll brush your hair for you."

"That sounds nice," Sissy says.

I sit there in my wheelchair and stare after them as they leave. Obviously she has some kind of Schizophrenia thing going on. *Wow. And what of her real family? Does she have any?*

I look over at Ray-Ban. He has three pieces of the puzzle left and is concentrating fiercely. *Did he even see what just happened to Sissy? Or has he seen it so many times it doesn't even faze him anymore?*

"Done!" He jumps out of his wheelchair for a split second before realizing he shouldn't be able to do that. He sits back down and looks around before returning his gaze to his finished masterpiece.

I wheel over and look at his puzzle. The castle is familiar. I remember seeing it on a tour of Scotland, a lifetime ago. I had a driver, an English guy named Paul, and we both loved castles. We stopped at each one we came to. This castle in the puzzle stood in all its greyness on a rocky point. Huge, waves broke against the cliff below. The sky was blue-black, ominous, like a storm was coming. I imagine the great hall awash in festivities with people dancing and drinking. Knights gnawing on huge bones of meat. Wenches wearing peasant blouses and pouring the beer. *And where am I?* Over there with the Minstrels.

Ray-Ban looks at me with eyebrows raised.

"It's beautiful." I say.

He looks back down at his puzzle. "Yeah."

I look at him, and he has disappeared himself, somewhere in the castle.

I imagine him as the king, his wheelchair now his throne.

"Wonder what it was like. To live back then. Jousting and sword fighting. Wearing all that armor."

"And corsets!" I add.

"And eating meat off the bones!" he says.

"Medieval barbecue!"

"Yeah. King Brisket."

"And Queen Coleslaw!" I add.

We both laugh at our stupid jokes so hard we almost fall out of our chairs. The tears run from beneath Ray-Ban's famous glasses.

We look at each other and smile.

"Ray, I was wondering about some of the others in here, like The Professor. He seems normal. Why is he here?"

"He had a stroke. He was pretty bad for a while."

"Was he really a professor?"

"Yep. English Lit. But then he left the university and became a novelist."

"Really? A writer? Wow. But he seems okay, now. Why is he still here?"

"No insurance. Bad divorce settlement. Guess his novels never did much."

"Maybe he should start writing again."

"May not have the inspiration anymore."

"Yeah, I can relate to that," I say.

"Maggie, as you know, used to be a model. She lived a jet-set life. Spent all her money. And now, as you also know, suffers from dementia."

"And Sissy?"

"That's one sad story." Ray-Ban looks like he is about to cry. "Her parents were alcoholics. Her father started sexually abusing her when she was a kid. Her mother looked the other way. I think she started living in a fantasy life to get through it. Family services finally came in and put her in a foster home. I think she went through about a dozen families over the years. She was abused by some of her fosters, too."

"Jesus. That poor girl. She's had such an awful life."

Ray-Ban shakes his massive head. "Yeah, people who do things like that ought to get the chair."

We sit there quietly for a while.

"If you're wondering about me," he begins, "my story is bad, but not that bad."

"Tell me."

He leans back in his wheelchair and closes his eyes. "Well, I'm from Detroit. Bad hood. Lotsa gangs. Was in some trouble as a kid. Nothin' bad. Mostly just stealin' cars. Finally got caught and spent some time in juvy. Scared the heck out of me. When I got out, I started going out for football. Found out I was really good at it. Well, I got a scholarship to UT. Then I was offered a contract with the Oilers. Played linebacker."

"No shit!"

"No shit," he says, smiling. "Then I was traded over to the Titans when Nashville bought us up."

"Really? You played for the Titans?"

"One game."

"One game?"

"I had the ball and was running down the field, and this guy comes out of nowhere and tackles me." Ray-Ban stops and looks at me. "I hit the ground hard. *Real* hard. I ended up in the ER. When I woke up, they gave me the news. I had broken my back. I was paralyzed from the waist down."

"My God! Ray, how awful."

"Yeah, I was pretty bad. My whole life was torn from me. I wanted to kill myself."

"I can imagine."

"Somehow, with the help of Jesus, I got through."

I lean closer. "But you're not paralyzed anymore."

He laughs. "No, but what am I supposed to do? Can't play ball anymore. They'd discharge me from here if they new I could walk. Then what? Get a job at Burger King and make $7 an hour. Who could live on that? Be homeless? Live at the mission? No. This is where I am for now, 'til I think of something."

I sit back. It's all so overwhelming; these wonderful people have no one who cares. We sit in silence for a while until my eyelids begin to feel droopy.

"Well, I'm gonna head back to lie down."

Ray-Ban nods. I leave him gazing down at his completed puzzle.

I pass Sissy's room. She is tucked in bed. Kelly sits on the edge of the mattress, brushing Sissy's blonde locks. I see Kelly's lips moving, whispering sweet soothing words to her. I smile and keep wheeling. My roomies are sleeping; the TV is blaring. I look at Morphine Drip. I make a decision and wheel over and turn off the TV. *Bliss.*

***

I am in Scotland. I am on a boat, a Ferry, on some lake in the Highlands. There are mountains. Big mountains all around. It is cold and the wind whips my hair back but I stand there and soak up the moment. Then the sun breaks out and engulfs me.

***

"Lunchtime!" Shanika whirls into the room and delivers our trays.

I look under the silver tray to reveal something that resembles a hockey puck. *Is it a hamburger?* I pick it up to inspect it. It is hard and black and cold. Next to it is a potato. Also, hard and black and cold. And a small wilted iceberg wedge. *Why even bother with the lid?* I try a bite of the puck. It almost breaks my teeth. But I am hungry and manage to eat it all.

"Hey!" Roomie number one says. "Why the hell is my TV not on?"

I am stunned. I didn't know she could talk.

"Did you turn off my TV?"

I am afraid to say anything.

"You keep your fingers off of my TV, bitch!"

Kelly comes in with our meds. "What's the matter?"

"Turn my TV back on!"

Kelly glances over at me and then walks over and turns on the TV. Morphine Drip glares at me, grabs the remote and turns it up even louder.

Kelly hands me my cup. I take the pill. She looks down at my tray. "Wow. Must have been pretty good, huh?"

"No, it was dreadful. But it's not like they deliver to this place."

"Actually, there is a pizza place that will."

I look at her. "Really? Pizza?" My mouth starts to water and I wonder how long one could live on Boost *and* pizza. Maybe indefinitely.

I ask her about the empty room, and she says she will look into it.

"Gotta go, sweetie."

The rest of the day I spend writing in my notebook. I start a journal and write everything that has been happening to me that I remember. I write about my new friends, Ray-Ban—the king of the castle—Sissy, Maggie, The Professor, Kelly and even Wooly Bully.

***

I wake up. It is dark. I must have slept through dinner and meds. There's no tray. I buzz the nurses station. "Excuse me. This is Jessie in room 104. I need my meds, please.

And I never got my dinner."

"We put your tray on your table. Ain't my fault you didn't eat it."

"Please, anything. A can of Boost. And I really need my pill."

I wait a good half hour and finally the thieving nurse comes in with something that used to be oatmeal in a former life. And the little white cup. "Here," she says and storms out.

I start to take the pill but notice that it doesn't look right. It looks smaller and thinner than usual. I take it anyway and eat the gray glob. It has a funny taste, but I am starving.

I lie back and try to go to sleep, but the pain doesn't go away. Doesn't even dull.

Maybe it was an old pill.

I decide to wheel down to the nurses station to see if I can find a different nurse. Maybe get another pill. There is no one around.

I start to wheel back to my room when I hear laughter coming from the nurses lounge. I stop and listen near the door.

"Well, I'm clearin' $300 to $500 a week here. Let 'em pay me $20 an hour. I make it up on all the meds."

"I switch aspirin for the Tylenol 3s."

More laughter.

Another voice. "I put a little blue food colorin' on a vitamin C and pass it off as

Morphine.

"Half these morons don't know what they're taking."

More raucous laughter.

"I just give 'em an empty cup first. Tell 'em they already took it. Most of 'em don't even know. Although I did have one argue with me about it last night. Guess she'll have the vitamin C, next time."

"Her piss is gonna be bright orange."

"At least she won't get scurvy."

More laughter.

"At least we have the smart ones who actually sell us their meds… I make up to $100 a pill."

I can't believe what I am hearing. I want to burst into the room. I am so angry, but suddenly I am gripped with fear. I long to be back in my bed. I turn my wheelchair away from the door. It squeaks.

"What was *that?*"

I start to wheel away, but the door opens, and the thieving nurse sticks her head out.

"You!" she screams. "What are you doing? Listening at the door? What did you hear?"

"N-nothing." I wheel as fast as I can. I hear her behind me.

She grabs my wheelchair and whirls me around. Her eyes are on fire with hatred. "If you dare say anything to anyone… It will be the last thing you ever say! I'll see to it. Now get the hell out of here!"

I wheel away as fast as I can.

"I will make your life a living hell!" she calls after me.

Back in my room, I shake uncontrollably, not believing what has just happened.

The thunder crashes outside my window. I draw the covers around me.

Make my life a living hell? Hell, I was already in it.

***

I wake with an alarming pain in my bowels. No way I can make it to the toilet.

I grab the buzzer. "Bedpan!" I yell into it.

No answer.

"Please! I need a bedpan!"

"Hold your horses!"

"Please! Hurry!"

Finally a nurse looks into the door and tosses a bedpan at me. It almost hits me in the head, but I am able to catch it. With much difficulty I get it beneath me, not one second too soon. I think I may have Krystal Burger beat on this one.

When I am finally done, I buzz the nurses station. Of course there is no answer. The steel of the bedpan chills my entire body. I buzz again.

"Please! This is Jessie. I'm done. I need someone to come get this from under me."

"Oh hello, Jessie." It's the voice of the thieving nurse. "Sorry. I'm a bit busy right now. Be there when I can. Give you time to *think* about things."

Oh my God! She is going to leave me like this.

I scream.

The nurse storms in. "Shut the fuck up! Shut the fuck up now or I'll shut you up myself!" She wrestles the pillow from beneath my head and holds it over me.

I look at her in horror.

She is going to smother me!

A moment passes and she puts the pillow down. She starts to walk away. "You buzz me again or yell, and I will be back to shut you up for good. Just say you died mysteriously in your sleep. End up in the morgue. Nobody will know any different or care, for that matter. Now, you can lay there in your own shit."

CHAPTER FOUR
The White Guitar

"Breakfast!" Shanika starts to put the tray down, but before she can, I grab the Boost.

"That's all I want."

She looks down at the rubber eggs and burnt toast. "Can't say as ah blame ya." She delivers the other trays to my roomies and leaves.

I open the can. Chocolate. My favorite. The stuff isn't really all that bad.

The memory of last night comes washing over me. I feel under me. The bedpan is gone.

Did I dream it? Am I losing my mind?

I grab the journal from under my mattress and start writing down what I can remember from last night while I can still remember it.

If it happened.

"Hey, sweetie." Kelly comes in and hands me a white paper bag.

"What's this?"

I open it to find a steaming Starbucks cup and a cheese Danish. The smell is intoxicating. I open the lid. It's a cappuccino. I almost cry.

"Kelly, thank you so much."

"No problem. Enjoy. And here's your pill." She puts the little cup down on my table and starts to leave.

"Kelly?"

She turns and looks at me. "Yes?"

"Kelly, I need to talk to you."

A worried look creeps over her face. "Did something happen last night?"

She sits down on the edge of my bed, and I tell her about the bedpan ordeal. About the nurse threatening me and holding the pillow over my head. And about the conversation I overheard.

She looks like she is aging in front of my eyes.

"Jessie, are you sure you didn't dream all of this? You are on a lot of medication. It can mess with your head. Your bedpan is clean and in the same spot it always is. These are incredulous accusations, Jessie. And you don't have any proof."

Ray-Ban wheels into the doorway.

"We're having a private conversation, Ray," says Kelly. "You'll need to come back later."

"There *is* proof," Ray-Ban says, wheeling towards Kelly. "I couldn't sleep last night, so

I decided to work on a new puzzle. I was on my way to the lounge when I saw the nurse go into Jessie's room. I heard her threaten her. Once I knew Jessie was okay, I got the hell out of there before the nurse saw me."

"My God." Kelly's face turns ashen.

"Kelly, I'm scared. Really scared. What are we going to do?"

Kelly frowns. "Okay. I'll visit the Director in person as soon as I finish work. I don't want to talk to him over the phone about this. Keep in mind that he may want to talk to you."

"Okay." I say, relieved that maybe we can get these nurses fired.

"Don't worry. I will take care of this tonight." She pats my arm. "But Jessie, Ray-Ban, please, for your own safety, do not tell anyone about this."

"I didn't hear nothin'," says Ray-Ban, wheeling out the door.

***

"Smoke break!" Layla's voice comes over the loudspeaker. "The morning smoke break will start in 15 minutes. Anybody wantin' to fill your lungs with black soot meet in the lounge in 10."

Why not?

I grab a $10 from my drawer to pay Ray-Ban. Maybe he can get me a pack of smokes when he sneaks out.

The lounge is filling up when I get there. Maggie is on the couch. She still has the same *Seventeen*. Ray-Ban is playing a game of pool with himself. He wheels around the table taking his shots. The Professor is filling his pipe. Sissy is nowhere to be seen.

"Hey," I say, wheeling over to watch Ray. He makes a solid side-pocket shot.

"You play?" he asks.

"Well, I used to. But I don't think I could play from a wheelchair."

He shrugs and goes back to his game.

I wheel over to the book and game shelves. I pull out the chess set and bring it over to our table. I look over at The Professor. He is watching me intently, his eyes wide with anticipation.

I smile at him. "I was thinkin', after smoke break, maybe you could give me a lesson."

"Well, of course! I would indeed be honored to give you a lesson, my dear."

"Cool." I look around again. "Where's Sissy?"

"Probably sleepin' in," Ray-Ban says.

I wheel over to Maggie. She looks a bit more distant today. "How ya doin' Miss Maggie?"

She looks up at me like she has never seen me before. "Do I know you?"

"It's me, Jessie." I say to a blank wall.

" I have to get to my shoot," she says.

"Maybe after smoke break, Maggie."

"Okay gang!" Layla calls out. "Let's go. We all file out to the porch. Ray-Ban, The Professor, Maggie and I are not in any hurry. I wonder if I should check on Sissy, knowing how much she loves to get outside twice a day.

"I'll be right back," I say to Ray. Then I remember. "Oh, here." I hand him $10. "Two for the lottery tickets and maybe you could get me a pack of cigarettes? American Spirit, ultra lights. Orange, please."

He takes the money, nods and wheels towards the door. Maggie and The Professor follow.

I wheel down to Sissy's room. I look in. She is still sleeping. I go to her bedside and shake her a bit. "Sissy?"

She looks up at me groggily. "Huh?"

"Sissy, it's smoke break. Wanna come outside?"

She sits up but doesn't open her eyes.

"Sissy?"

She lifts her arm up as if reaching for something like an imaginary butterfly.

I watch her. Her eyes are still closed, but her arm stays in the air. She is drugged. On something strong. Thorazine. Something like that, anyway.

I remember some guy giving it to me one time, years ago. I was out of it for days. Bad medicine. I take her arm and put it by her side.

"Okay, Sissy, I'll see you later."

She doesn't respond. I wheel back out to the lounge, outside and down the length of the porch, passing all the smokers. I try to pass through all the people sitting and people leaning against the railing. "Excuse me," I say, but no one moves. "Excuse me. Can you just move a bit so I can get through?" I look at the rail. Morphine Drip is there smoking. She looks at me, and I swear she shows her teeth like an angry dog.

No one moves.

The Professor comes my way. He gets behind my chair and shouts, "Move!" Like magic, the seas part. He wheels me down to the end and parks me so I can see the woods.

"Thanks, Profess—I mean Mr. Jones."

"Morons," he mutters under his breath and refills his pipe.

"Pretty, isn't it, Maggie?" I wheel next to her and follow her gaze to the woods.

She doesn't answer, lost in her world of high fashion. I try to picture her as a model. I can see it. Her cheekbones are high, her eyes almond shaped and a vibrant green. I bet she was beautiful.

As if she can read my thoughts, she looks at me. "I was once very much in demand." Tears brim her eyes.

"Maggie, you are still very beautiful." The Professor says.

The two of them goo-goo eye each other. I smile.

Something going on here?

"Look at all those pretty flowers," says Maggie, eyeing some dandelions in the grass. "I think I'll go pick some." She heads down the steps.

Ray-Ban appears and sits down in his wheelchair. He hands me my cigarettes. The Professor is there for me with his silver lighter.

We all smoke in silence and stare out at the woods. In a few minutes Wooly Bully saunters out, followed by Miss Pearl.

"Wooly!" Ray-Ban calls. Wooly runs across the expanse of grass, up the steps and onto Ray-Ban's lap. I look back out. The black cat keeps her distance.

"Blackie!" I yell.

The black cat looks up and starts coming across the lawn. She gets to the steps and looks at us, at Wooly being petted. Then at me.

"Blackie?" Is that your name?" The cat looks at me again and meows.

Ray-Ban laughs. "Whatsamatter? Don't like Miss Pearl?" He laughs so hard that Wooly Bully looks at him almost quizzically.

"Blackie, come here." I put my hand down.

Ray-Ban frowns at me. "Well ya gotta lure her over. She ain't gonna come for nothin'. Here." He gives me a piece of soggy bacon from breakfast.

"Do you really think she'll eat this?" I ask with a smile.

As soon as I put my hand down with the flaccid meat, the cat is there. She is gentle, doesn't try to grab it from my fingers. She sits down and very slowly starts chewing on one end as I hold it. When she is done, she meows at me. Then she starts to wash herself.

"Smart cat," The Professor says.

"Yeah, I like little Blackie," I say.

"Her name is Miss Pearl! Not Blackie!" yells Morphine Drip from her spot.

"Well, I think she just changed it!" Ray-Ban yells back.

I look over at Maggie. She is not where she was a few minutes ago.

"Where's Maggie?" I ask. We all look around, but she is gone. "Did she go inside?"

"Last I saw, she was picking those dandelions over there," says The Professor. His voice holds a hint of alarm.

"She musta' snuck away while we was talking'," says Ray-Ban. "Maybe I should go take a look." He starts to get up when suddenly Layla appears on the porch. He pretends to have been readjusting himself in his chair.

"Okay, smoke break is over, y'all. Let's go."

"Shit," mutters Ray-Ban. "This is not good."

"We gotta tell someone," I say. "She can't be wanderin' around the streets by herself."

We all go in, and Layla locks the door behind us.

"Layla, I think Maggie might have slipped off," I tell her.

"What?" she says. "Just now?"

"A few minutes ago."

"Shit!" She runs out of the lounge towards the nurses station.

"They'll find her," says The Professor. "She's done this once before."

"I can't believe we didn't see her slip off," I say.

"Well, usually we keep an eye on her," he says, dropping his gaze to the floor.

"Well, hey, what about that game of chess?" I ask, hoping to perk up his spirits.

"All right." His voice lacks the excitement it held before.

We set up the game.

"Okay," he says. "First, you must learn the chess pieces and what they mean and what they can do. You must think of the chessboard as a battlefield."

He shows me the pawns, the knights, the bishops, the king and queen and how they can move. He reminds me to always guard the queen.

"So, ready to try one, my dear?"

"Sure."

I learn quickly and actually enjoy it. I even get the hang of thinking a move or two ahead, trying to get The Professor to make a dumb move and nab one of my pawns. But he never falls for it. He wins each game, of course. The first two go rather quickly, but the third game lasts almost a half hour.

When Layla returns we ask her about Maggie, but she is still missing.

How'd she get away that fast? Not like she's a 20-year-old track star.

"Well, I'm gonna go lie down," I say. "See you guys later. And thanks for the lesson, uh, Mr. Jones."

"Maybe again tomorrow?"

"Sure thing." I say and head down the hallway.

I get back to my room. Same old TV blaring, same old stench. I head back out to the nurses station.

Layla, Kelly and Shanika are all talking on the phones.

"Kelly?" I ask.

She holds the phone away from her ear a minute. "Yes, Jessie?"

"I was wondering about that empty room. If you talked to anyone to see if I could switch?"

"Jessie, not now. We have a major crisis on our hands." She puts her ear back to the phone.

Miss Maggie. She really is missing.

I wheel back to my room, my cell, and get into bed. I just want to sleep. Maybe I will dream of some faraway place, with mountains and oceans and soft tropical breezes. Get away from here for a while. To be free again. To be happy again. To be *me* again…

***

I am in my car singing along to the radio. I go down a big hill. I try to slow, but my brakes won't grab. I try and try and slam my foot down.

Still nothing.

I am in a house. A rundown adobe. I am lying on a couch covered in bandages. There is a wooden pipe sticking out of my throat. *Some kind of ancient trach.* People mill around. *Native Americans.* One keeps checking on me. A man with a long black ponytail and glasses. For some reason, I think he is a doctor. He checks my IV and the thing in my throat from time to time. I want to ask him where I am but can't talk. I think I hear a few of the Indians saying they have to get to Rapid. *Rapid City?* That the Feds are on their way.

And then all hell breaks loose. There are sirens in the distance and the Indians run around grabbing things and heading out the door. I hear car doors slam and engines roar to life and tires squeal. The ponytailed one comes up to me and begins to take the thing out of my throat. I try to stop him.

"You're not going to make it anyway," he says. But he leaves the trach in place and runs out the door. A few minutes later, I hear a car pull up. A policewoman rushes in and points a gun around the room.

"It's okay. We're going to get you to the hospital." Somehow she gets me into the police car and puts a modern trach in my throat. She speeds off.

***

The dream was so real, even though it didn't make any sense.

I had been out to Pine Ridge a few times. The Pine Ridge Reservation is in the southwestern corner of South Dakota. A few friends and I had a grassroots organization for a while called HONAR. (Helping our Native American Relatives). We would hit yard sales and ask the people to donate their toys, warm clothing, anything. Then we'd put on concerts and auctions to raise the gas money. U-Haul would even donate huge trucks for us. At first, we only had one connection, a woman who worked as a maid for the Tribal Council in the town of Pine Ridge. The corrupt Tribal Council members always took what they wanted for their families and then sold the rest of the stuff to the Indians living at the outposts. So we started delivering to the far outposts of the "res."

It was a beautiful but desolate place. One of the families we *were* able to help was that of famous medicine man Vernell Cross. It was a life-enriching experience to see the smiles on their faces. The children grabbed toys, and the women held up clothing.

My friends and I worked at the Recycle Center in Nashville for a week. The center rewarded us by filling our truck with everything from kitchen sinks to toilets, carpeting, doors, windows and roofing material. Vernell was able to add another room to his house where he, his wife and at least a half dozen children lived. Another time we managed to fill half the truck with turkeys for Thanksgiving.

I lie in my bed now, wishing I could be out there, making another run to the res. Maybe if I ever get out of here I could get HONAR back together.

"Lunch, ladies." Kelly breezes in. "Hey, Jessie." She smiles to me, as she delivers the trays to my roomies. I watch her. Krystal Burger is still snoring away. I look at Morphine Drip. She glares at me. She watches Kelly as she puts a tray on my table.

Kelly sits down on the edge of my bed.

"I've called the Director, and I am going over to see him when I get done with work tonight."

"Really?" I look at Morphine Drip who is still staring at us. I start to tell Kelly not to say anything, but before I can get the words out she continues. "I didn't want to talk on the phone about it, so I am going to his house to tell him. If what you heard was true, then by all means we have to do something about it. I just want you to know that this should all be settled in a few days."

"Oh, Kelly. Thanks."

She pats my arm and takes the silver lid off my plate. Beneath it is a bit of rice covered with something that looks like glue.

"What *is* it?" I ask.

"Chicken over rice."

"Where's the chicken?"

There is also another wilted iceberg wedge and some neon green Jell-O. And, of course, the Boost, which I grab and hungrily gulp down.

"Did they find Maggie?"

"Yes, she is safe and sound. Someone on the next block called the police and said there was an old woman sitting on her porch swing. I guess she just decided to make herself at home there."

"Well I'm glad she's okay. Oh and Kelly, what about the room?" I gesture for her to come closer. "That woman," I glance over at

Morphine Drip, "is giving me the creeps. And the evil eye."

Kelly looks down at me. "Well, they have someone coming in tomorrow. I just found out a while ago. I am sorry, sweetie. But, I was thinking, what about if you room with Miss Maggie? We are going to have to put someone in there with her. I think you would be a fine candidate."

"Really? That would be heaven. I like Maggie."

"Okay, let me see what I can do. Maybe we can get you moved in there before I leave."

"The sooner the better, Kelly."

"Okay, but gotta run for now." She smiles and heads out to deliver Bubba's glue over rice to all the other victims.

I watch as Morphine Drip gets up and walks out of the room. Guess she doesn't like glue either.

Krystal Burger seems to love it. She uses both hands to shovel in fistfuls of the goo. I think she is getting more on herself than in her mouth. It is disgusting, and I feel like I want to vomit. On that note, she looks over at me and lets out a fart so sour it brings tears to my eyes. I don't even throw on my robe. I fling myself into my wheelchair and get the hell out of there before the place blows.

I wheel down the hallway to look in on

Sissy.

Still sleeping.

The next room is Maggie's. She is sitting up in bed looking at a magazine.

I poke my head in. "Maggie?"

"Why, hello, dear. Please do come in."

The room smells like lilacs. And even though I don't like flowery scents, it smells a lot better than where I had just come from.

"Hi, Maggie. How ya doin'?"

"Well. I'm doing just fine, Jessie. Thank you for asking."

Wow. She remembers my name.

"Maggie, would it be okay with you if I room with you?"

"Well of course it would. I would love the company."

I look around. There is no TV, only a radio by her bed with some nice light jazz playing.

Heaven.

"Okay, I just wanted to ask you first. I'm gonna see if I can move in this afternoon."

"Well that would be wonderful. We can look at magazines together."

"That would be nice," I say and start for the door. I want to get moved *now*—before they move someone else in here and I am stuck with the roomies from hell.

"See you in a bit then."

I wheel down to the nurses station.

Kelly is talking to a patient, but she waves

me over. "Go start packing up, Jessie. We've got permission for you to move in with Miss Maggie."

"I don't have much, Kelly. It won't take long."

I am ecstatic. I get back to my room. Krystal Burger has let out a few more ripe ones, and I am tempted to go back to the nurses station and ask for a mask. Morphine Drip is still gone. No love lost there. I spend the next hour putting my few things together. A change of pajamas. My robe, socks, some books, a toothbrush, a hairbrush and that's about it. Funny how much my life has been simplified since the accident. I used to have so much stuff. Well I still have stuff. At my house. I just don't have any stuff here. Don't need it.

Then I remember my journal. I reach under the mattress, but it is not there. I search everywhere.

Nothing.

Weird.

Kelly comes in holding a giant box. "Hey, you got a big package, Jessie."

"Wow. It *is* big." I look for a card. I cannot find one, and there is no return address on the package. "I don't know who it's from."

"Maybe there's a note inside."

I tear open the box. Inside is a hard shell guitar case. I open the case. Inside is a white guitar. But there is no note. Just the most beautiful guitar I have ever seen.

"WTF?"

"No note? How strange. What a gorgeous guitar. Do you have any idea who sent it to you?"

"No, Kelly. I have no idea."

I pick up the guitar. It is a Taylor. Looks custom made. It is so white, it glistens. It is inlaid with Mother of Pearl. I try a chord. It is in perfect tune. The sound is beautiful. I try another chord, then another. The sound resonates through the room.

"Wow," I say, admiring its beauty.

"Maybe you have a secret admirer," Kelly says with a wink.

I laugh and shake my head in disbelief. "Yeah right."

"Well, let's get you moved into Miss Maggie's. I have more rounds to make." Kelly grabs my garbage bag full of stuff.

I get in the wheelchair, and Kelly places the guitar on my lap. We head down the hall to my new room.

Maggie is sitting up, with a big book in her lap.

Kelly helps me unpack, and I lie down on my bed with my guitar next to me.

"Oh I do hope you will play for me," Maggie says.

"Maybe sometime, Maggie. I haven't played in so long. Kelly can you put this in the closet for now?"

She puts the Taylor in its case and tucks it away.

"Okay, gotta go. I'm off early today," she says. "Have fun, ladies." She looks at me. "I'll talk to you tomorrow, Jessie. I'm going to take care of this."

***

"What is that book?" I ask Maggie.

"It's my portfolio. Would you like to see it?"

"I would love to, Maggie."

She gets up and hands it to me. The first picture I see is of a young, maybe 20-year-old Maggie. Her hair is golden blonde. Her green eyes stare off into the distance. A close up. I flip through the pages. Maggie selling perfume. Maggie selling lingerie. Maggie selling shampoo. There are also many runway photos. She is the most beautiful woman I have ever seen.

"God, Maggie. What a knockout."

She smiles at me. "Thank you."

"Hello? Anyone home?" The Professor knocks gently on the doorframe. "May I come in?"

"Of course," we both say at the same time. He hands Maggie a red rose.

"Oh, James! It's beautiful."

James?

The Professor pulls a chair next to Maggie's bed. "No more dandelions, Maggie."

Maggie sniffs the rose, her face beaming.

"Have you seen this?" I ask, gesturing to the portfolio.

"Oh, yes. But I think Maggie just gets more beautiful with every passing day."

Definitely something going on here.

I wonder if I should wheel down to the lounge to give them some privacy. But just then the loudspeaker blares through the hallway.

"Smoke break. Smoke 'em if you got 'em. Fifteen minutes everybody."

Cool. I get in my chair and start wheeling towards the door. The happy couple follows.

We pass Sissy's room. She's still asleep. When we get to the lounge, Layla comes running up behind us. She grabs hold of Maggie's arm. "Sorry, Miss Maggie. You can't go. You have to stay in your room."

"We'll watch her," I say.

Layla shakes her head. "No. Sorry. We can't take the chance of her wandering off again. Come on, Miss Maggie. I'll walk you back to your room."

They disappear down the hall.

"This is going to kill her." The Professor says. "She loves going outside."

I nod. There is nothing to say.

Smoke break comes and goes. Ray-Ban is

sullen. Wooly and Blackie don't even make an appearance.

***

A male nurse I have never seen before comes in with our dinner trays. He is young, white, maybe mid 20s. He is burly and beer bellied, sporting dingy gray scrubs and a mullet haircut. Short in front, long in back. Awful all over.

He sets down Maggie's tray on her table and then delivers mine.

"What up?" He leers at me.

Great. A white guy speaking Ebonics. Just what I need.

"Where's Kelly?" I ask.

"She had to leave early."

I can feel his eyes on my breasts.

I remember she was going to the Director's house to talk to him about the meds—and everything else.

"Oh yeah."

He reminds me of a ferret. Beady little eyes.

"I'll be on all night tonight. If there's anything you need, Red. Name's Joey. Just buzz if you need me."

I look at him. His eyes finally migrate up from my chest to reach my face.

"Just buzz if you wantin' some company?"

I'd rather take a bullet.

"I *doubt* it," I mutter under my breath.

He chuckles and nods. "You might want to think about being nice to me."

"I'll think about it." I glare back at his smirk.

He shakes his head and starts for the door, but stops short and turns around.

"Yeah, you *do* that. Think long and clear about it, bitch."

Bitch?

I sit there, stupefied. Was he insinuating I sleep with him in order to get my meds? Or food?

Food.

I finally open the silver lid. Something gray and foul smelling, like rotten meat. I put the lid back on. Purple Jell-O. No fruit. No vegetables. I grab the Boost and savor it. I've been living off of it for two days now.

Maggie is still sleeping. No need to wake her up for this meal. Suddenly I remember the pizza place Kelly told me about. I grab the takeout menu she had left for me. I start to salivate as I skim it over. It lists 12 different pizzas. Spinach and goat cheese. Meat-lover's paradise. I decide to live it up with "The Hawaiian," ham, pineapple and extra cheese.

I grab some coins and my credit card and wheel down to the payphone in the hall. I call and order the pizza. Extra large, so I can share with Maggie. I ask if they can deliver it to the nursing home. They tell me yes, and ask for my credit card number. They do not need an address or directions. No surprise there. They could probably run their business on this place alone.

I wheel back to my room, wishing I had my journal. I never did come across it packing up. I pick up a paperback I had borrowed from the lounge. A James Patterson novel I had not yet read. I get so engrossed in the book, I almost forget about the pizza. I look over at the clock. Forty-five minutes have passed. They said a half hour.

I read another chapter.

Shit.

Still, no pizza. I get back into the chair, grab more coins and start down the hall. I call the pizza place. They tell me they delivered it an hour ago.

I wheel down to the nurses station. Mullet and another new male nurse—this one with a shaved head that glows—are busy looking at *Hustler.*

"I'd like to play those bongos," Cueball says.

"You could suffocate in there," says Mullet.

"Excuse me," I say.

They both look at my breasts.

"I ordered a pizza and never got it."

"That so?" Mullet says.

"I called them back, and they said they delivered it an hour ago."

Mullet shrugs. "Dunno nothin' 'bout no pizza."

"Well, maybe somebody else got it. Could you check?"

"Ain't no pizza come in here," Mullet says.

I turn and start to wheel back to my room.

"Next time, hope she don't put none of that fuckin' pineapple on it," Mullet says. "I hate pickin' that shit off. Pineapple on a pizza. Fuckin' broad is wacked."

I wheel back to my room, my stomach gurgling, head spinning, heart racing. I am going to starve to death in here. Sissy was right.

Maggie is awake. Our dinner trays are still on our tables, hers untouched, as well. I tell Maggie about the pizza.

"I'm so hungry, Maggie."

She looks up at me and goes to her closet. She pulls out a paper bag and rifles through it. She hands me a baggie. Inside is a sandwich. American cheese on rye bread.

"It's the only cheese that will keep without being refrigerated," she says. "But it does have some Dijon on it."

"Oh, Maggie, thank you."

It is the best sandwich I have ever tasted. I devour it in a minute flat. Then she hands me a box. It is a pastry box. I open it. Inside is a chocolate cake. It has musical notes on it and *Happy Birthday* scrolled in pink icing.

I start to cry. "Maggie, this is the sweetest thing."

"Well, I didn't find out it was your birthday 'til today. Sorry."

"We don't have a knife to cut it."

"But we do have plastic spoons." She takes the purple Jell-O out of our bowls and dumps it over the gray stuff. Then she fills each bowl with cake. Chocolate with chocolate frosting and butter cream filling. It is delicious.

"My God. This is so good! Maybe we should save some for the gang."

"Good idea," she says through a mouthful of cake. "Right after this next bowl."

We refill our bowls and laugh. I eat until I am stuffed. We devour the whole thing.

"They say you can't have your cake and eat it, too," Maggie muses.

"Well I'd rather eat it than have it."

It's not very funny, but we laugh anyway.

I lie back, satiated and content. And maybe a bit high on sugar.

We listen to the radio. Dianna Krall singing, "Glory of Love." Then Bobby Darin crooning, "Sea of Love." Chocolate cake and jazz. All I am missing is a glass of Pinot Noir.

CHAPTER FIVE
Where the Hell Am I and
How the Hell Did I Get Here?

"Meds!" The thieving nurse comes in. I watch her as she gives Maggie her pills. She walks over to my bed and hands me the paper cup. I take the blue pill from her and examine it.

She shoves a glass of water at me.

"What the hell are you looking at?"

I roll the pill back and forth between my fingers. The blue food coloring begins to come off.

"Take it! I don't have all day!"

I gulp down the pill.

What the hell? At least it's Vitamin C and not a horse tranquilizer.

I think of Sissy again.

The nurse hands me another pill. A small white one.

Is it the zombie pill that's been knocking everyone out?

I hold it under my tongue.

The nurse leaves. I spit out the living dead pill—I'll save it for a rainy day or the zombie apocalypse. I take the real morphine pill out of my pocket. I had saved it from the lunchtime delivery. I open the Patterson book and start to read, but my mind is elsewhere and I cannot concentrate. Maggie is sleeping soundly.

I hear yukking coming from the hall and see Mullet and Cueball walking by. Mullet looks in, sees me, and air puckers a kiss.

Gross.

I go back to the book, but still can't concentrate. I lie there and hear yukking coming from down the hall.

I climb into my chair.

The yukking is coming from Sissy's room. Her door is closed.

I try it.

Locked.

I hear a voice from inside. "Ooh baby, ooh baby. That's right. Suck it for me."

I sit there paralyzed for just a second. Then I turn into a banshee and bang on the door.

"Open this door you fuckin' assholes or I'll scream bloody murder."

"Fuck off, bitch!"

"Open this door now or I'll call the police!"

The door flings open, and Mullet and Cueball stand there tying up their scrub pants.

"You want to join the party, Red?" Mullet asks.

I glare at him and push through the door.

Sissy is lying in her bed, propped up on pillows. Her long wheat hair spreads out over them. She looks at me through vacant turquoise eyes and smiles.

"Hi Jessie," she says.

Her eyes are glassy.

Is she stoned?

"Sissy, are you all right?"

She looks fine. She does not look frightened or upset at all.

"Sissy, did they hurt you?"

She looks perplexed. "Hurt me? For heaven's sake. No. Joey and Donnie are my new friends."

She hands me a box wrapped in pink paper tied with pink ribbon. "Look what they brought me!"

I open the box. I pull out a sheer pink teddy. I look at Mullet and Cueball. They stand by Sissy's bed with legs spread and arms crossed.

"Isn't it beautiful?" Sissy asks. She holds it up for me to see.

I try to give her a smile.

I have to tell someone about this. Just not now. I start to wheel out of the room when I hear Mullet behind me.

"See there, Red. Everybody's cool.

Everybody but you."

When we're in the hall, I lose it. "If you ever touch her again, I will kill you."

"Ooh, I'm soooo scared. Whatcha gon' do? Stick me with a fork?

I wheel into my room and slam the door. I am so mad. Maggie is still asleep. I lie there fuming.

***

I am on a stretcher, some kind of metal gurney in a curtained off room. I am alone and strapped down. My doctors come in. One is the ponytailed Native American. The other is a tall blond with spectacles and a receding hairline. They are talking about me but they don't seem to know I can hear them.

"She's still got a pulse," Glasses says.

"Let's give it another few minutes," Ponytail says.

She's lost a lot of blood. Shouldn't be long now."

"I'm gonna need that liver pretty soon. They're already prepping him."

"The kidneys, liver, and heart," Glasses adds.

"We're gonna get rich on this one."

"I can't decide if I want to retire in Hawaii or the Bahamas," Ponytail says.

"Better looking babes in Hawaii."

They look at me once more.

"You just lie there quietly and die," Ponytail says. They leave.

I try to move but I am strapped in tight. I can move my foot, the one not covered in gauze and bandages. I move my left foot vigorously. Maybe if I can make myself bleed, someone will see fresh blood and know I am not dead, that I am not about to die.

I take my foot and start scraping the bottom of my foot against the metal gurney. Back and forth. I don't feel much pain but I can feel it is starting to bleed. I feel wetness. More and more.

A nurse comes in. "Oh my God! Doctor, come quick!"

A different doctor rushes in.

"Oh my God, This is fresh blood. She is not dead. I think she is trying to tell us she is still alive. Get her to the OR immediately. Now! Get Tressler up there for her other foot. I want a team. The best. Get her hooked up to blood and morphine now."

He rushes out of the room.

I open my eyes. I see the nurse standing over me. Long auburn curls. Kelly. My guardian angel.

***

"Room check." Layla struts in wearing a pair of lavender scrubs and a lavender wig to match.

"What?" I ask, shielding my eyes from the morning sun.

"State is coming today," she explains. "Gotta check, make sho' y'all don't have no contraband."

"Contraband?"

"Yeah." She rummages through our drawers. "Uh oh. This yours?" She holds up a plastic razor.

"Yes. But you can have it. I don't really need it in here."

"Got that right." She smiles and moves on to Maggie's dresser. "What's in here?" She looks into the paper sack that holds Maggie's sandwiches. "No food allowed in the rooms. Sorry." She tosses the sack into a garbage bag.

"Layla. Please let us have those last two sandwiches," I beg.

She looks doubtful. "Okay, but eat 'em now, before State gets here."

She continues into the bathroom. "No shampoo either. You have to ask for it at the station when you want to shower."

"But that stuff is awful. I can't get the knots out of my hair."

"Sorry." she says. "Okay y'all are clean."

Jeez Louise.

Here we are with nurses stealing patients' medications, male nurses sexually abusing female patients, food not fit for a dog—and they are worried about shampoo.

What am I going to do, wash myself to death?

"Yo, breakfast." Shanika is all dressed up in what looks like a new pair of scrubs. Magenta with pink ribbons.

I don't even open the lid. I grab the Boost and reach for my cheese sandwich. Maggie is still asleep, so I stash hers under her pillow. I head for the lounge, gobbling down the sandwich with one hand and wheeling with the other. Not an easy task.

The gang minus Maggie is there. Sissy is on the couch, drawing in a sketchbook with crayons. The Professor is in his reading chair. Ray-Ban is at his usual spot at the table.

"Hi y'all," I say.

"Hi Jessie!" Sissy says. She is wearing her pink terrycloth robe, but I can see the teddy sticking out from underneath.

"Good morning, Jessie," says The Professor. "Did they find anything on you?"

"Yeah, they confiscated my razor and my shampoo. Why would they want my shampoo?"

"There was a patient here that used to sneak into rooms and drink it."

I shake my head and wheel over to Ray-Ban.

He looks up. "Hey."

"Hi Ray. Here's my dollar. And one for Maggie."

He pockets the money. "Cool."

There is a new puzzle in front of him. He has only just started it. I look at the cover. It is a beach scene. Multicolored fishing boats are lined up on white sand. Turquoise water and a turquoise sky make up the background. Hard puzzle. Lotsa blue. Sounds like a song.

You got lotsa red hot lovers, I got lotsa blue.

Whatever. My songwriting skills definitely need some practice.

"New puzzle, huh?"

"I don't know where to start. Too much blue."

Ooh, that's even better.

Too much blue.

"Maybe do the boats first."

"Good idea." He begins separating all the colors into individual piles.

"How is Miss Maggie doing?" The Professor asks.

"She's still sleeping."

I am craving a cigarette. I glance at the clock on the wall. Just after nine. Smoke break time. They are late.

The loudspeaker comes on.

"All of those wishing to fill their lungs with carcinogens, please make your way to the lounge."

Another joker.

A few patients shuffle in, all looking like zombies. I feel like I am in *The Night of the Living Dead.*

Layla marches in all businesslike. She

unlocks the door, and we all file out. The "gang" brings up the rear. We take our spots at the far end of the porch. Ray-Ban looks around, gets up and disappears around the corner of the building. I know there is a Kwik Sak a block away. That must be where he goes to get the cigs and lottery tickets.

"Sissy, how ya doin'?" I ask.

She smiles but her eyes are vacant. "Great. I feel great."

I look out at the woods. I see Wooly Bully and Blackie at the edge.

"Wooly! Blackie!" I yell. They both look up and start to come, but suddenly they turn and run back into the woods.

The front porch door opens, and Layla come out, followed by a man and woman.

State?

"And this is where we have smoke break," Layla says. "Twice a day. Fifteen minutes."

"Smoke break?" I hear the woman say. "Well, that is something that we will have to put an end to. This is a nursing home, not a recreation center. Patients are supposed to be getting healthy in here."

"Smoking is not good for your health," the man adds. He's probably about 50, but with his bald head and bad comb-over, he looks older. Stuffy. He is dressed in an ill-fitting suit that looks like it came from Goodwill.

The woman is chunky and wears too much makeup. She's wearing a bad combination of blue eye shadow and red lipstick. Her gray hair has been dyed brown, but not lately. Her roots are showing. Her black pantsuit is also ill fitting and looks like it belongs back in the '80s.

"Everyone, may I have your attention?" Layla says. "This is Mr. Shitz and Miss Nogutmik—"

"Shmitz," says the man, "with an 'm'."

"Oh sorry," says Layla. "Anyway, they are from the state. They are here because of the complaints being made. They will be setting up new rules and help us enforce the ones we have. I would like everyone to give them your full cooperation. Then, they will decide whether or not they will close us down."

I watch as they start down the length of the porch. I look over at Ray-Ban's empty wheelchair. *Where is he?*

They stop to listen to a few of the patients' complaints.

Nurses using terms of endearment, no doubt, when all of this other shit is going on.

Then, they continue towards us. Just as they are about to round the corner, I wheel over in front of them.

"Hi!" I say, all smiles. "So, y'all are from State?"

They stop abruptly and look me up and down.

"Yes, we are," says Miss Nogutmik. "And who are you?"

"My name is Jessie. I'm a musician. I was in a very bad car crash a few months ago. I just want to say, I have a few complaints."

She looks at me impatiently. "Yes?"

"Well," I begin, pretending to think for moment. "Well, we need to have Marvin back."

"And who is Marvin?" she asks.

"Marvin was our cook here. He was really a great cook, too. He made meatloaf and mashed potatoes, and really good fish—"

"Well, we had to let some staff go."

"But no one else can cook like him."

"Miss, this is not a gourmet restaurant. This is a state-run nursing home. I am sorry if you do not like the food here, but there is nothing more to be said about this matter. Now if there is nothing else…"

I think about telling her about the male nurses. Mullet and Cueball. But I decide against it. It will be my word against theirs. I must keep talking, though. If they go around the corner, they will see Ray-Ban's empty wheelchair, and that will not be good.

"Well, also I would like to have my own shampoo," I add.

"Definitely not."

I hear a wheelchair pull up next to me. My heart skips a beat.

"And who are you?" asks Miss Nogutmik.

"I'm Ray. And I got nothin' to say."

"Well then, I guess we are done here," she says. She walks back down the length of the porch.

"Oh," she says, turning back to glare at me. "For your information, no one else has complained about the food."

Probably because they have all turned into zombies.

"Smoke break is over," Layla yells from the front door. "Everyone back inside."

We file back into the lounge. Ray-Ban heads over to his puzzle to escape into a paradise with fishing boats and turquoise water. I want to go there, too, so I wheel up next to him at the table.

My spot.

"Thanks," he mutters, not looking up.

"No problem." I mutter back. I glance over at Sissy who is coloring again.

"Well, Jessie, maybe you would be so kind as to join me in a game of chess," The Professor says.

"Okay," I say, reluctant to leave the fishing boats.

We set up the chess pieces on the table across from Ray-Ban's puzzle.

"This is *not* a good idea." Nogutmik has suddenly appeared. "Someone could choke on these pieces. I want this game removed now!"

I look at her in amazement. "No, please.

You can't do that."

"Oh no? Watch me!" She uses her arm to sweep the chess pieces to the floor. Then she grabs the board and tosses it into the trash.

"And puzzles? I think not!" She starts to reach for Ray-Ban's boats.

I swear I see his eyes glow red.

"Back off, lady!" He covers his puzzle with his huge arms.

She jerks back as if she has been slapped. "Well, we'll see about all this." She turns and almost runs back to the safety of Layla and Mr. Shmitz, who are standing in the other section of the lounge.

"Yo! Refreshments." Shanika whirls in with her cart and ribbons but stops midstride when she sees the state people. She pauses for a minute to collect herself before continuing silently over to our table.

"Ah din' know them was here," she whispers.

"They threw out our chess set," The Professor says.

"Ahm sorry 'bout that. Ah knows how you like to play." She pours us some lemonade from a plastic pitcher.

I glance over at Sissy, sitting alone on the couch. "Sissy? Why don't you come color over here with us?"

She remains glued to her spot. She doesn't look at me. Instead she looks around and above her.

The spiders?

I start to wheel over to her, just as she jumps off the sofa, flailing at the air around her.

"No! No! No!" she screams. "They are making a web around me!"

"Sissy." I try to grab her arms. "She tears at the air, thrashing at an invisible web. Then her arms fall to her sides and stay there, tight, like they are glued to her torso.

"What the hell?" Mr. Smitz says. Layla runs to Sissy's side, and Sissy goes limp in her arms. She picks Sissy up like she weighs no more than a rag doll, and carries her out of the room.

Shanika stands at our table, mouth agape, the pitcher still in her hands.

"Shouldn't she be in a mental institution instead of a nursing facility?" Smitz asks.

"That's what this is," Ray-Ban says under his breath.

"What the hell was that all about?" Miss Nogutmik asks.

A voice curses from down the hall. "Hell! Hell! Hell! Fuck! Fuck! Fuck!"

Toenail.

He is so loud that Shanika drops the pitcher of lemonade, which, of course, splatters all over Miss Nogutmik.

"Now look what you've done!" she yells at Shanika. "I just had this suit cleaned!"

"Ahm so sorry, Ma'am. Toenail. I mean

Mr. Tonell scared me."

"What the hell is wrong with *him?*" Miss Nogutmik asks.

"He has Turrets. He can't help it," I try to explain.

The cursing continues so loud it is deafening.

"Well, he needs to be locked up, as well. I am definitely going to report all of this." She starts for the door but turns back and looks at Mr. Shmitz. "Come on. Our time is done here! What are we waiting for?"

Silence.

I reckon someone has calmed Toenail.

I look at The Professor. He looks very old. Very tired. Shanika has gotten a towel and is mopping up the lemonade. Layla comes back into the lounge. Her shoulders are slumped and she dabs a tissue at her eyes. She walks slowly over to our table. The three of us, The Professor, Ray-Ban and I watch her. Something is wrong.

"Layla, I know it's sad that the state is closing us down, but it'll be all right," I say.

"It's not about the state," she says between sobs. "It's Kelly."

My heart skips a beat. Then another. Then it starts racing.

"What?"

"She had a car accident after she left work yesterday." Layla pauses to dab her eyes. "She died."

A million screams go off in my head at once.

"No!"

"What happened?" Ray-Ban asks.

"Her brakes went out. She hit a telephone pole. Died instantly."

Her brakes went out? Just like mine had. No, no, no. It couldn't be true. Not Kelly.

Kelly with her auburn curls, her three children, a dog and two cats. And a loving husband.

No, no. Not Kelly.

I shake uncontrollably. Layla grabs me, and I fall into her arms.

"Shh, now," she says, but her sobs are as loud as mine.

Ray-Ban wheels up to us. I can see a lone tear fall from under his sunglasses. He takes my hand and holds it in both of his.

"The Lord works in mysterious ways," says The Professor. I can see that he is crying, too.

I look at him and take his hand with my other hand. He looks defeated. I look down to the floor and see the chess pieces scattered about.

Defeated, fallen soldiers. Dead soldiers. Just like us.

CHAPTER SIX
Physical Therapy

Shanika comes in with our trays. No twirling.
I think of Kelly.

*Did I dream that whole thing? Please, God, let it
be so.*

Shanika is wearing black scrubs. No
ribbons. Bad sign.

"It's true, isn't it?" I ask. "Kelly. I didn't
dream it did I?"

Shanika sits down on my bed. "No, you
didn't dream it." She looks at me. "You
needs to eat. You look skinny."

I realize that I am famished. I reluctantly
open the silver lid. A boiled egg, burnt toast
and two soggy pieces of greasy bacon. I
crumble the egg into the toast and manage to
get it down with the Boost. Amazingly, it
doesn't taste half bad.

"Gotta go," she says and shuffles out of
the room.

I look over at Maggie. She is not eating,
not sleeping, just staring into space. A Sissy

look.

"Maggie?" I ask. "Are you all right?"

She looks at me, confused. "Who are you?"

"It's me, Jessie, Maggie."

"Jessie Maggie," she repeats.

Oh no. Has her dementia gotten worse? Or is it the meds?

She looks at me and then looks at the wall. She raises a shaky, vein-lined hand and points to the closet.

"Do you want something from the closet, Maggie?" I ask her.

She nods.

I get out of bed and wheel over to the closet. I open it. It is full of vintage dresses and gowns. Mostly from the '60s. Really cool stuff. Purple and black paisley mini dresses, a white full-length Nehru-collared Indian dress, and a pink poodle skirt that Sissy would go bonkers for—if she weren't already bonkers.

"Wow. You have some great clothes, Maggie. Do you want one of your outfits?"

She shakes her head. I look back inside.

What does she want?

Then I see it nestled in the back of the closet.

"The guitar?" I ask her.

She nods. She wants me to play the guitar. I carefully lift it onto my lap and wheel over to her bed.

She smiles.

"I haven't played in a very long time, Maggie. I'm afraid I may be a bit rusty."

She frowns at me slightly like she is saying, "Just play the damn thing."

I strum an E chord. The tone is beautiful, loud and rich. It rings out and fills the room. I play an A. Then a B. Your standard blues progression. I start to hum along. I think of Kelly and the words start pouring out:

Auburn curls, eyes so blue,
sweetest person I ever knew...
A heart so kind,
her words so true,
how could this ever happen to you?
My tears fell hard when I got the news.
Now I'm lying here with Kelly's blues.

When I finish, I look over at Maggie. She has tears in her eyes.

"I'm so sorry, Maggie. Kelly was wonderful. We will all miss her."

The loudspeaker comes on. "Smoke break! Anyone wishing to help pollute the earth, please make your way to the lounge."

"I'm gonna go smoke, Maggie." I put the guitar on the bed, grab my cigarettes and start down the hall.

The Professor is in his chair, filling his pipe. He looks up and smiles at me. A half-hearted smile. No sign of Sissy.

Ray-Ban is at the table, his puzzle in front of him.

"Hey," I say.

"Hey," he says back. The puzzle is coming along. There are yellow, red and white fishing boats now lined up on the golden sand. No sky, no sea; too much blue. As I look closer I can see that there are actually two different color blues. The sea is a greener color. I start to tell him that but decide against it. I know how protective he is with his puzzles, and he will probably figure it out anyway.

Layla comes in, also wearing black scrubs. And a black wig. Cleopatra style.

"Hi Layla," I say. "I like your hair."

"Thank you," she says, touching the wig. She starts towards the door, and we all get in line and file out. The three of us take our spots at the far end of the porch. I hand Ray-Ban a few dollars.

"For Sissy and Maggie," I say.

He looks around a second, takes the money and vanishes out of sight.

I take out a greasy napkin and unwrap the bacon. I look out at the woods but don't see Wooly Bully or Blackie.

"How is Miss Maggie?" The Professor asks.

"Not that good, really. She stopped talking."

He merely nods, sucking long on his pipe.

"This is really getting messed up," I say, taking out a cigarette. He lights me up.

"I agree. They are closing us down. The place is already on the market. Two mil."

"I wonder what they will do with it."

"Probably convert it into little boutiques. Maybe a hair salon, a dress shop, an expensive bakery."

"Charming."

I know this part of East Nashville is becoming a boomtown. I bought my house 18 years ago—before the yuppies moved in, and then the "hipsters." I liked it better when it was me, the rednecks and a few musicians.

Ray reappears, sits down in his wheelchair and gets out his soggy napkin. "Wooly Bully! Come on, boy."

Like magic, the two cats appear at the edge of the woods.

"Blackie!" I yell. The two come running.

Wooly rubs up against Ray-Ban's leg, and to my surprise, Blackie rubs against mine. We give them their bacon. Then Blackie jumps up into my lap. I stroke her. For a wild, feral cat, she is in good shape. Smooth, silky black fur. Beautiful green eyes. She licks my hand as I pet her. It feels so nice.

"She really has taken a shine to you," says Ray-Ban as he strokes Wooly. He has curled up in his lap.

I smile, and he smiles back.

A rare moment. If it could only last.

Layla appears at the door and announces that smoke break is over. As I wheel down the length of the porch, I pass Morphine Drip, who is stubbing a cigarette out in a plant.

Class act.

"It's all your fault, ya know," she hisses.

I look at her. "What are you talking about?"

"You know damn well what I'm talking about. Tryin' to fuck up everything we got goin' on here. I was making damn good money on my meds. Living in this shithole, but putting away a grand a month. Then *you* had to go poking your nose into everything, writing in that stupid notebook, tell-tailing to that fuckin' nurse. Hope you're happy. And you better just keep that trap of yours shut if you don't want to end up in the morgue." She pushes in front of me and almost slams the door in my face.

I sit there shaking and stupefied. The world starts spinning around me. I think I am going to pass out.

The Professor grabs my chair and gets me inside. "Are you all right, Jessie?" he asks.

I cannot answer. I cannot breathe. I shake my head.

"I'll wheel you back to your room."

My mind is racing.

Could Kelly's accident be my fault? Unless it wasn't *an accident.*

Maybe someone tampered with her brakes. Then I remember my notebook. It had disappeared. I had written everything down. I remember the way Morphine Drip looked at Kelly and me when Kelly was telling me she was going to see the Director right after work.

Oh God, no.

"Jessie?"

I look up from my bed. A tall, dark-haired male nurse I have never seen before is standing at the foot of my bed.

"I'm Mike. Your physical therapist. I've come to take you to therapy.

"What? Physical therapy?"

"That's right. Come on. Hop in. I'll wheel you down."

"There has got to be some kind of mistake," I say.

"No mistake," he says, looking at a chart.

"I don't want to go."

"Well, if you ever want to walk again, I suggest you get in this wheelchair so we can get you out of it."

He seems nice enough, but I am still hesitant.

"But I am just getting used to the wheelchair."

He sighs. "What will it take?"

"A hot fudge sundae." It was the first thing that came to my mind.

"Done," he says.

I get into the chair, and he whisks me off down the hallway. We get into the elevator, and I am again suspicious.

"Where are we going?"

"To Ben and Jerry's."

"Huh?"

"To the physical therapy room, silly girl."

We get off the elevator, and he steers me down a long hallway. At the end of the hall is a room. He pushes me in. It looks like a torture chamber. I start to wheel myself the hell out of there, but he grabs my wheelchair.

"You want that ice cream or not? Come on. It's not as bad as it looks."

There are a few other people in the room, and a few other nurses. I let out a sigh of relief. He is not going to strangle me or bludgeon me with an ax and dump me off at the morgue after all.

The room is full of all kinds of contraptions, treadmills, weight machines, giant mattresses, and all kinds of balls and colorful free weights.

"Yikes," I say.

Mike wheels me in front of two bars with a walkway between them.

"Okay. Grab the bars."

I do.

"Okay. Now try to pull yourself up."

I try but can't.

"Try again."

I try. But still can't do it.

"Hmm. Guess we're going to have to work on some upper body strength."

I try again, and again, and finally manage to pull myself up. I am very wobbly.

"Great!" says Mike, like I've just reached the summit of Everest.

"Now, try to take a step."

I try, but can't do it. My arms feel like they can't support my weight. I fall back into the wheelchair.

"Again," he says.

I give him an exhausted look.

He looks sad, like he really wants me to do this. So, I try again. I manage to get myself up, but fall back every time. This goes on for several minutes.

"Okay. That's enough," he says.

"But I didn't even get to take a step."

"I didn't expect you to. But you tried. You did great. Let's start to build those arms up."

"Okie dokie."

Okie dokie?

I don't think I have ever said that in my life.

He laughs and wheels me over to the free weight shelves. He takes out two purple free weights and demonstrates what he wants me to do with them.

"Try to do 10 of these," he says, curling his arms first and then he holds the weight above his shoulder and raises it overhead.

"And then ten of these. Three reps each."

I admire his muscular arms. He is quite the looker. Dark brown hair, beautiful eyes, and a body that could make a nun blush.

I take the weights and do as I am told. I think I would do anything for this man. I would do a hundred reps if he wanted me to, maybe even a thousand.

The exercising feels good, but I am tiring fast.

"Okay, let's go over to the mats."

"What? Are we going to wrestle?" I feel myself go red the minute it's out of my mouth.

"Leg exercises," he says with a smile.

"Lie down on our back."

Yes, sir!

I lie down, and he takes my left leg in his beautiful hands and starts to lift it.

"Does that hurt?"

"No."

He switches to the other and takes off my sock.

"Okay. Now I'm going to massage your calves. Tell me if it hurts too much."

Never.

I close my eyes as he rubs my left calf. It does hurt, but in a good way. Then he does the right one. I am in heaven. I never want it to end.

"Wow. How'd you get this scar on the bottom of your foot? It looks pretty fresh."

"Scar? I don't know."

The dream.

"Okay." he says. "That's good for today."

"My back kinda hurts today," I say.

Mike chuckles. "Oh it does, does it? Well okay, turn over."

I do not believe my good luck. He massages my neck, my shoulders, my back. I keep letting out big sighs, like I'm having multiple orgasms—which maybe I am.

He laughs. "You're gonna give everyone the wrong idea."

And you're never going to have to bribe anyone with a sundae.

He finally pats my arm. "Jessie? You still with us?"

I was almost asleep.

I look into those big brown eyes, and with every bit of resolve, I climb back into my chair.

Do you need any help getting back?" Mike asks. "I have another patient."

I almost feel jealous. "No. I can manage."

"Well, I'll see you on Thursday then."

"Thursday? I don't even know what day today is."

He smiles. "Day after tomorrow. I'll come get you after lunch."

"Okay. Thanks."

I wheel myself back to the elevators and press the button.

My mind is so preoccupied thinking about

those brown eyes and strong hands I hardly look up when the elevator doors open. I start to wheel myself in.

"Hey, Red. What up?" Mullet says. The doors close. He flashes me a smirk. "So, we finally get to be alone."

I push the first floor button.

He presses a button. The elevator STOP button.

"What's your hurry, Red?" He leans into me.

"Get away from me, you asshole."

"You know you want it, bitch. Just suck it for a second. You'll like it."

"Don't you dare touch me." I push the first floor button again.

He presses the STOP button again.

"We could be here all day, Red. Better get with the program."

I hit the button again, and the elevator starts to move.

Thank God.

"Okay, bitch. Have it your way. Sissy is a lot younger and prettier than you anyway. And she *likes* her lollipop."

I am fuming. I want to kill him.

The doors open, and I wheel out of there and down the hall like a wild woman. A few startled nurses glance up at me as I race down the hallway. Maggie is asleep when I get back. I crawl into bed and curl up in the fetal position.

***

I am in a field of wildflowers. A beautiful white stallion comes rushing towards me, then stops and nuzzles me. I jump on his back. He snorts once and takes off in a full gallop. The sun is a big amber ball on the horizon. The sky is vivid shades of pink. The horse races through the meadow. His mane whips behind him. I hold on for dear life. But I am not scared. I feel free.

CHAPTER SEVEN
Mad Woman

I awake to the sound of someone screaming and cursing. Not Toenail. It's a woman's voice.

"Fuck you! I am not staying in this loony bin! You can't do this to me! Get me the hell out of here. Now!"

I sit up, fully awake. The screaming is getting closer. *Uh oh.*

Suddenly, all the lights go on in our room as three paramedics rush in with a 30-something woman. An elderly couple follow, looking nervous and exhausted.

"What's going on?" I ask one of the paramedics.

"Got you a new roommate," he answers.

The woman looks at me and spits in my direction. A huge wad of green slime hits the foot of my bed. "Fuck you!" she wails at me.

I watch as they wheel a bed into the corner and strap her in. She thrashes and curses at the top of her lungs.

The elderly woman walks over to my bed. She is maybe 60, although she looks like she has had a facelift, and could be in her 70s. She looks very straight-laced in her Chanel suit and Hermes scarf. She doesn't have a platinum hair out of place.

"This is my daughter, Tiffany," she says, a scowl on her plastic face. "I hope you won't give her any problems." She walks back to her daughter's bed.

Give her *a problem?*

I look over at Maggie. She is also wide awake with a worried look. I sneak a look at Tiffany. She does *not* look like the daughter of this country club woman. She looks like a meth head—very gaunt, pale and unhealthy. Her jeans are ripped and grungy. Her dirty blonde hair really *is* dirty, and stringy, and her pupils are so dilated I cannot tell what color her eyes are.

The parents are trying to console this mad woman, to no avail, stroking her hair, and whispering soothing phrases. "It's for your own good. You'll only be here a few days."

Then you'll be transferred to a real loony bin.

"I am *not* staying in this nut house! Not for one fucking night! You get me the hell out of here, right the fuck now!" Mad Woman screams.

The paramedics file out, shaking their heads, leaving the lights on. Her parents are still fussing and cooing over their daughter.

Layla comes in, carrying a small white pill cup and some water.

"Tiffany, I have some medicine for you. It will help you relax."

"I'm not taking any fucking medicine!"

"Yes you are." Layla tries putting the pill in Mad Woman's mouth. "It's Valium. You need to quiet down, now." Layla smiles calmly. Then, in a heartbeat she jumps back. She holds her hand in front of her as it bleeds profusely.

"Oh my Lord. She bit me!" Layla runs out of the room, holding her hand.

From down the hallway, I hear Toenail joining in on the chorus of cuss words. I look around, stunned. Maggie buries her head under a pillow. My ears ring, and a massive migraine rushes at me like a freight train.

The parents are still fussing over their precious daughter, who continues to curse at them.

Layla re-enters the room with a syringe in her hand, followed by Mullet.

"No fuckin' way!" screams Mad Woman.

She thrashes so much I am sure the restraints will break free. Mullet holds her as still as he can while Layla gives her the shot.

I cannot take anymore. I get into my robe and wheelchair and wheel down to the lobby.

To my surprise, Ray-Ban is sitting in front of the TV watching an infomercial. Someone is explaining how to make 20 different meals using one single household appliance.

I wheel over next to him. "I didn't know you were into cooking."

He smirks at me and looks back at the TV.

"I got a new roommate," I tell him.

"Yeah, I heard. Couldn't help but hear."

"Yeah, so much for sleep."

He smiles. "My room is next to Toenail's."

I laugh. We watch in silence as the man shows us how to prepare a stuffed chicken breast on the gadget.

"She called us all loonies," I say.

"Here long enough, she may be right."

"Ray, I'm scared. This place gives me the heebie-jeebies at night."

"Yeah, me, too."

"I wonder if Kelly ever got to talk to the Director. She thought I was dreaming up everything... Thank goodness you overheard that nurse threatening me."

Ray-Ban nods. "I think they said she was out in Belle Meade when she had the accident. That's where he lives."

"But was it before or after she saw him?"

Ray-Ban shrugs his football shoulders. "We don't really know."

"Do you think it *was* an accident?"

"Jessie, I am sure this will all be figured out soon enough. You need to lie low for now."

"Thank God for Mike."

"Mike? You know Mike?" he asks, an eyebrow raised.

"Well, yeah, he's my physical therapist."

"Oh."

"Why? You go to him, too?"

"Nah, I just know him from around. Good guy."

"Yeah. He's sweet."

There goes his eyebrow again.

"You sweet on him?" he asks.

I sucker punch him on the arm. "Ray!"

"Well?"

"Well, maybe a little. But don't you *dare* tell him."

Ray-Ban laughs. "Scout's honor... We gonna have a lot of secrets between us, girl."

"Just remember. Play it cool. *Real* cool. Don't start any shit."

"I'll try, Ray."

"Every little thing gonna be all right."

"Bob Marley."

"You know it, girl."

We sit, deep in thought, in silence.

Silence!

The screaming has stopped. All is quiet. I feel drained, sad and sleepy.

"Well, I think I'll go back and try to get some sleep. Thanks, Ray."

He nods, staring back absently at the infomercial.

Back in my room, Maggie is asleep, head

still buried under her pillow. Mad Woman is snoring loudly. The parents have left. I turn the lights off and crawl into bed.

***

Shanika whirls into the room with our breakfast trays.

She sets mine down. "Morning, Jessie, sleep okay?"

"Not really."

I watch as she delivers the other two trays. Mad Woman is sitting up, glaring at her.

Shanika puts a tray down in front of her. "You're the new girl. Tiffany, right?"

Shanika unfastens the restraint on Mad Woman's right hand. Mad Woman reaches for the silver lid. "What the hell is this shit?"

"Scrambled eggs and SPAM sausage," answers Shanika, backing out of the room.

As soon as she leaves, Mad Woman looks at me. "What the fuck are you looking at?"

I look away and open my Boost.

"Fucking SPAM? No fucking way!" She grabs the plate and hurls it at me. It misses my bed, but splatters all over the floor. "Fuck this. Where the fuck are my stupid parents? They better bring me some real food."

As if on cue, her parents walk into the room and step over the glop on the floor.

"Tiffany, honey, how are you feeling this

morning?" asks Country Club. She sets down a beautiful vase full of red roses.

"Like shit. I hope you brought me some fuckin' food."

"Of course, sweetheart," answers the woman.

The father pulls up a chair for the woman and puts a large brown paper sack on his daughter's table. He is fit for his age, balding, dressed in a green Polo shirt, and khakis, like he is about to hit the greens as soon as he is out of here.

"We got you a cappuccino, bagels with cream cheese and lox, and two blueberry muffins."

The smell is intoxicating. I wipe the drool off my lips.

Mad Woman takes a bite out of the bagel and spits it out. "Yuck. This tastes like shit. There's fuckin' dill on the lox!"

"Please, Tiffany. Do you always have to use that four-letter word?" Country Club asks.

"What word, mother? Dill?"

"Well, maybe you'll like one of the muffins. Would you like me to butter it for you, dear?" asks Daddy Dearest.

"I *hate* fuckin' blueberries. Don't you know anything?"

"Well, I know you like coffee," says Country Club. She opens the lid and hands the cup to her daughter.

Mad Woman takes a swig. "It's fuckin' cold, *mother!*" She throws the cup against the wall.

"Tiff, please," begs Daddy Dearest. "We're only trying to help."

"We only want the best for you, darling," adds Country Club.

"This is all your fault! Putting me in this hellhole. I'm sick of you. Get the fuck out and don't come back 'til you are taking me out of here. And take your fuckin' food with you!"

"Honey—"

"Out. Get *out!*"

Daddy Dearest puts an arm around Country Club. "Come on, honey. Let's leave her alone for a while." He grabs the sack of food, and starts for the door.

"Excuse me," I say, mustering all my courage for the sake of starvation. "I would love those bagels and muffins."

They stop short and glare at me.

"You need to mind your own, business, missy," says Country Club.

"Maybe we should see about getting her a private room so that girl stops bothering her," adds Daddy Dearest.

I lie back.

Then Mad Woman buzzes the nurses station. "I need to go to the bathroom," she says.

"We'll send some one right in," answers a

sing-song voice.

Guess the parents are stroking someone's wallet.

The loudspeaker comes on. "Smoke break! Smoke 'em if ya got 'em."

I throw on my robe and vault myself into the wheelchair.

"Where the fuck are you going?" Mad Woman asks.

"Smoke break."

I wheel out the door. I hear something shatter behind me. I look back to see the flower vase in a million pieces, the beautiful roses scattered amongst them. A terrified Maggie is standing there, too, and she pushes me furiously down the hall.

***

"So, how's the new roommate working out?" asks Ray-Ban after he has returned from his jaunt and we are all seated on the porch smoking peacefully with the wildcats.

I shake my head. "I kinda feel sorry for her, in a way."

Ray-Ban raises his famous eyebrow.

"Well, she seems like she is spoiled rotten, and is *not* a nice person, but who knows? She is rebelling against *something.*"

"A $500 weekly allowance?" Ray-Ban jokes.

"Is that who I heard screaming last night?" asks Sissy. "Your new roommate? I couldn't get back to sleep. And then Toenail started in."

I laugh. "Yeah, me neither."

Ray-Ban takes out a piece of the SPAM sausage and tries giving it to Wooly, but the cat just looks at him as though he has lost his mind.

"We're all doomed."

"No we're not!" Sissy says.

We all look at her.

"We have each other! We're family!" She smiles, reaches over and strokes Wooly.

I look over at The Professor, who is smiling adoringly at Maggie, who is smiling the same smile back at him. Then I look at Ray-Ban, who is absentmindedly stroking Wooly with a crooked, half smile curling his lips.

God, I love these people. I truly love these people… These strangers who are now my family.

I feel lucky. I smile, too.

We file back in when smoke break is over. We all seem to be lost in our own thoughts, but a peacefulness engulfs us.

"Peace y'all," I say and wheel back to my room, the smile still on my face and my spirits are high.

"Thanks a lot, bitch." Mad Woman hisses when I get back to my room. I see my reverie breaking up into a million star molecules, like a kaleidoscope, and floating away. I want to grab them, but they are gone.

I don't answer. I just want to get back into my bed and go back to sleep, whatever that is.

I turn the wheelchair into the room.

"You went outside for a *smoke*?" Mad Woman asks.

I crawl into my bed.

"Why the fuck didn't you tell me?"

I pull the blanket over my head.

"Did you ever think that maybe, just *maybe*, I would have liked a smoke break?"

I crawl deeper.

"Hey, you. *Bitch*! I'm talking to you!"

Deeper. Can I make myself disappear completely under the comfort of my covers?

I try like hell. I want to fade away. Completely… Forever.

And then I hear her, sobbing softly. At first, a catch of her breath, a quick quiet "Huhh…" But then they come on, one after another, until they are an army against her.

I poke my head out a little and look over at her. Her head is buried in the pillow, and she is crying uncontrollably. I throw the covers back and wheel over to her. I stroke her hair.

"Hey, hey… It's all right."

More heart-wrenching sobs.

"Tiffany? It's okay. It's gonna be okay. I'm sorry I didn't ask if you wanted to go for a smoke. We can go later. Okay?"

Mad Woman's head turns and yellow eyes

glare up at me.

"Fuck you!"

I jump back. She looks feral. Poisonous.

"I was just trying to—"

"What? Fuckin' help? Get the fuck away from me, you fuckin' moron!"

I wheel out of the room as she screams vulgarities after me. The hallway is alive with nurses and patients, but my mind is somewhere else. I feel like I am being torn apart, limb by limb, nerve ending by nerve ending, cell by cell. I keep wheeling but there is no escape. I wheel on and on and on. Hallway after hallway.

***

I wake up in bed. How I got here, I am not sure. But I am here. Safe under the covers.

I peek an eye out and look over at Maggie. She's sleeping, her head buried underneath her pillow. I look over at Mad Woman's bed. It is empty. I peek the other eye out. Yes, definitely empty.

I get out of bed and wheel toward the bathroom. As I get closer to the door, an awful smell comes drifting my way. My heart leaps.

Is Mad Woman in there? Did she kill herself?

I open the bathroom door and almost gag. There in the middle of the floor is a huge pile of steaming poop.

I wheel out and into the hallway, holding my hand against my mouth. I see Layla behind the nurses desk.

"Hello, Jessie. What's wrong?

"That girl is gone. And there is a big pile of shit in the bathroom."

"Good grief," says Layla, rushing down the hallway.

In the room, I watch as Layla cleans up the pile wielding a swath of paper towels in one hand and using the other to cover her nose.

"Did she leave?" I ask.

Layla deposits the towels in a plastic bag and shakes her head. "No, she's out on the porch having a smoke."

"A smoke? But it's not smoke break."

"Well, Joey's out there with her."

"Mullet?" I ask.

She just looks at me.

"How come she gets to go out whenever she wants?"

"Because her parents are very wealthy and told us to give her the royal treatment."

"Well, I can see how appreciative she is leaving you to clean up her shit."

"That's enough, Jessie. That girl has been through a lot. You may want to try a little compassion."

I wheel out of the room and into an empty lobby. I go over and try the door.

Locked. I look outside and see Mad Woman smoking with Mullet, laughing, his hand on her thigh.

I try to hear what they are saying, but cannot. Then I watch as Mad Woman's hand goes to Mullet's crotch. They are both laughing and smiling, and now, Mullet's head goes back and I see him jerk.

Enough.

I feel sick. I wheel out of the lobby just as I hear the door open.

I get back in bed, and pretend I am sleeping. I hear Mad Woman come in and then her radio turn on. I hear her search through the dials until she settles on a rap station. The lyrics are obnoxious and crude. I wonder how people can listen to that stuff.

"Tiffany, can you turn that down?" I ask.

It's deafening. I feel like my head is going to explode. I get up, climb back into my wheelchair and head to the lobby. I lie down on the couch and am asleep, instantly.

***

The nursing home is eerily quiet, and I almost don't want to leave the lobby. But I am famished, and I wheel back toward my room, hoping I have not missed dinner. To my relief, I see Layla at the nurses station.

"Layla, am I glad to see you. I think I missed lunch."

She looks up with concern.

"Yes, I tried waking you a few times, but you looked like you needed to sleep. I saved you something."

She reaches down and hands me a tuna salad sandwich, which I open and start to eat right there.

"Thank you," I say between bites and wheeling back to my room.

The lights are out, the radio is turned off, and I crawl into bed. I don't know what time it is, what day or even what month it is. I don't care. It doesn't matter.

***

I hear moaning coming form somewhere in the room. I look around and see Mad Woman's bed moving slightly. With the light of the moon coming in, I make out Mullet on top of her.

It doesn't take long before I hear him climax.

"Oh, girl, I like the way you fuck."

"Yeah, well, you better stick to our plan and get me the fuck out of here."

"Yeah, okay. I'll take you out for a smoke, and you can do what you want. Lemme go see if the coast is clear."

With one eye open, I watch Mullet go to the door and look out. "Get dressed. Hurry up, and don't forget my money. I'll be right back for ya."

I watch Mad Woman get dressed and throw a few things in a plastic bag.

"I know you're not sleeping," she says. "You better not say anything, bitch… If you know what's good for you. I'm paying Joey big money to make sure you don't cause any trouble."

I ignore her.

Joey returns, and together they sneak down the hallway.

I can't believe my good fortune.

CHAPTER EIGHT
Concert from Hell

Ominous clouds hover above the tree line. I am having a smoke with the gang on the porch. We are all in a sour mood. Wooly and Blackie have taken up their usual spots: Wooly on Ray's lap and Blackie on mine.

All of a sudden, three good-looking men come up onto the porch and have a look around. I look at them with surprise. They are the guys from my band.

Holy shit!

They spot me, wave and walk over.

"Jessie girl!" they say in unison.

We exchange hugs and kisses, and I introduce them to the gang.

"Guys, this is Charlie, Bobby and J.D. They're the guys from my band."

Charlie and I had a long tumultuous affair. He's tall, blonde and blue-eyed. I look up at him now from my wheelchair and can't help but want to jump his bones. We agreed to finally break up after realizing we were better off just being friends. It still hurt, though, and to cope with the split, I married the first guy who came along.

Big mistake.

Bobby with his sliver hair is a looker, too. We've always been close. J.D. is a really funny guy, and I love him dearly in a brotherly sort of way.

"I know you didn't want visitors, but we bribed one of the nurses," J.D. says.

"What? With Lortab?" I joke.

I think about how horrible I must look and wish I would have had a warning so that I could have put on some makeup or at least run a brush through my hair.

Bobby can read my mind. "You look great," he says.

"Yeah you do," adds J.D.

"Thanks," I say. "But you're not very good liars."

They look a bit nervous.

"We got a present for you," Charlie says. "We called here last week and asked if we could do a concert here."

"Really? But I can't sing. My vocal chords are all messed up from the accident."

"We'll sing for you," Bobby says. "We got a lot of new songs we want you to hear."

Something in my stomach turns over.

Probably too much Boost.

Layla calls that smoke break is over and the concert is about to begin. We file back inside, and Sissy I grab the sofa.

The stage is set up. There are three mics in front—one set a lot lower than the others.

I grab J.D.'s arm. "J.D., there are three mics. I can't sing yet."

"We have a new singer," he says.

"Must be a real short guy."

"Actually, it's a chick."

I watch in horror as she struts up to the mic. She's got tits only someone other than God could have produced. She is dressed in a leopard print mini skirt, a halter top that reveals a silver navel piercing, fishnet stockings and stilettos. Long blonde curls cascade down her back.

Extensions.

"Hi y'all. I'm Kitty and these are my cats. We're 'Kitty and Cats' and we're gonna play you some of our songs. I hope you will enjoy them. Ready, cats?"

I feel myself turning green. Not from envy. I fear I may have to wheel myself to the nearest toilet. She has one of those little girl voices that I hate. And she dances—not in rhythm—while caressing herself.

Somehow I make it through the first song, and the patients applaud as if it were a Springsteen concert.

"This next song is so close to my heart," says Kitty, touching her silicone breast. "It's a song Jessie and Charlie wrote called, "Wherever You Are." She goo-goo eyes Charlie.

Gag.

I sit through it anyway with tears in my eyes. It was *our* song. Me and Charlie's. Next, Charlie sings an anti-war song he does so well. Then Bobby and Kitty sing a duet that he and I used to do together. Kitty doesn't know how to sing harmony. She sings in unison with Charlie, their voices blending like oil and water.

"Wow. They're so good," Sissy says.

I throw her a dirty look.

The concert from hell continues for another 40 minutes. The longest of my life. Thankfully, Kitty only sings a few more songs. Then she spends the rest of the time beating on a tambourine.

Out of time.

When they finish, the patients give them a standing ovation. Well, the ones who *can* stand, anyway.

I sit and pretend to clap, but really, I'm just bringing my hands together gently without making a sound.

Bobby and J.D. start breaking down their gear and hauling it out.

Charlie makes his way over to me. "Well, what did ya think?"

"Wow. Speechless. Brought tears to my eyes."

He catches my sarcasm and chuckles.

"You know she's just temporary."

"Oh…yeah…sure."

I look over at her. She is selling T-shirts and CDs and signing autographs at a nearby table.

"You did a CD?" I ask, my mouth dry.

"Well it's really an EP. Only six songs. You want one?

I laugh. "Oh sure. Love one."

When Kitty finishes at the table, she struts over to me.

Oh God, no.

"Jessie!" I'm so thrilled to finally meet you. I love your songs! I hope you don't mind me singing some of them. I can't write too good, but Charlie is teaching me."

God, I want to strangle her.

"Good luck with it," I say, wanting to mean it. But it comes out sarcastically.

"We have a lot of gigs booked," the brat continues. Even a tour in Holland."

"It's called the Netherlands," I correct her. "Holland is just a part of the Netherlands."

"Oh. Well, whatever," she says, looking over at the table where more patients have gathered. "Oops. Got some more CD sales. Better go.

"EP," I mutter as I watch her strut back to the table.

J.D. and Bobby walk over to me.

"Thanks, guys. That was so sweet," I tell them.

"I'm glad you enjoyed it," Bobby says.

"Enjoy? Did I say I enjoyed it?"

J.D. gives me a hug. "Jessie, it's so good to see you. You know, Kitty is just temporary." He leans in close. "The more temporary the better. When you get out, we'll start up again."

"Sure, cool."

"Don't worry, sweetie," says Bobby. "No one can replace Jessie James."

"Well, we better go. We got another gig in a few hours," Charlie says.

"We'll see you when you get out," adds J.D.

Sounds like I'm incarcerated.

I exchange hugs and kisses with the guys and watch them walk out. Kitty hooks one arm through Bobby's and another through Charlie's. J.D. turns and gives me a thumbs up. I wave back.

I wheel back to my room with tears spilling down my cheeks. I feel selfish. Here they came to play for free for me and the other patients, and I am being so ugly.

Maggie gives me a worried look.

"I'm okay, Maggie," I say and get into bed.

I pick up the EP. On the cover is a picture of Kitty sprawled seductively on a wide tree branch in the woods. She's wearing her leopard attire. The "Cats" are nearly hidden in the background amongst the trees. I hurl the EP against the wall. Unfortunately, it doesn't break.

CHAPTER NINE
Endless Days

Maggie is getting worse. She has ceased talking altogether. She has also stopped using the bathroom and is wearing diapers. She has also stopped feeding herself.

I haven't seen Sissy except for the few times I have stopped in her room. She is heavily tranquilized.

The highlight of my day is the one smoke break we get when I get to see Ray-Ban, The Professor and the cats. Unfortunately, they cut the evening smoke break we used to have. We usually don't even talk. Ray makes his quick trip to the Kwik Sak, and we feed Wooly and Blackie.

What a life.

I have lost a lot of weight. When I looked in the mirror the other day I hardly recognized myself. I used to be kind of pretty, but now I look gaunt, skeletal.

Twice a week I go to physical therapy. I

still have not been able to walk on the parallel bars. Mike seems frustrated with me. But I cannot do it. I have no strength, and maybe no desire. I just don't care anymore.

Autumn has come, and I can see the leaves falling outside my window. I lie on my bed and watch them for hours.

I play the white guitar, but not enough. It still hurts my fingers. I have started another journal and have written down everything that has happened here. I keep it under my mattress.

Mike has managed to get Maggie and me a TV. It's an old black and white and only gets six channels, but Maggie seems to enjoy it. Right now, there is an old re-run of *Bonanza* on, which Maggie loves.

"Oh, Maggie. There's Adam. I bet he's your favorite."

She looks at me and shakes her head.

"Little Joe?"

Again she shakes her head.

"Hoss?"

She almost laughs.

"Oooh. Ben."

She smiles.

"Yes, he *is* very handsome."

At least she can still understand some of the time.

There is a new nurse, Chenille, who has replaced Kelly. Well, not *replaced* her. No one could replace Kelly. Chenille is a short, stocky woman about my age. She is not very pleasant, always has a scowl on her face.

She enters the room with our lunch trays. She sets them down on our tables and then goes over to the TV and changes the channel to a soap opera. She pulls a chair over to Maggie and starts to feed her.

"Hey," I say. "We were watching *Bonanza.*"

"Too bad," she huffs. "I can't miss my soaps."

She spoons canned peas into Maggie's mouth. Her eyes remain glued to the TV, and the peas go all over the place.

"Watch what you're doing," I tell her. "You're missing her mouth!"

"Shhhh!"

Maggie picks a pea off her chest and eats it. I am getting angry.

"Why don't you let *me* feed her. You can go watch your soaps in another room."

"Can't," she says.

I wheel over to the closet and get out the guitar.

I start to play it, as loud and raunchy as I can.

Rock and roll. Baby!

"Shut up! I can't hear my soap."

I play even louder, wishing I had a Marshall amp I could plug into.

Chenille turns up the volume on the TV.

General Hospital. How fitting.

If they only knew what really went on, they'd have a soap opera horror show.

I start singing as loud as I can.

"I like that old time rock 'n' roll…"

An old Bob Seger song.

My voice is rusty and I can't hit the high notes, but I don't care. I wail on, anyway.

"Won't go to hear 'em play a tango…"

Chenille glares at me and flips off the TV.

"I'd rather hear some blues or funky old soul…"

"Fine," she snarls. "Have it your own way. You can both starve." She grabs our trays—mine still full—and storms out the door.

I look at Maggie. She is using her tongue to try to get the mashed potatoes on her chin into her mouth.

I put the TV back on *Bonanza* and wheel over to her. I gently push the mashed potatoes onto her lips. She licks them.

"I'm sorry, Maggie. Tomorrow I'll give Ray-Ban some money to get us food at the Kwik Sak. Even if it's crackers and canned cheese."

I sit there next to her, and we watch the rest of *Bonanza*. Little Joe has gotten himself into some trouble, and the Cartwrights are coming to the rescue. I wish they would come to mine.

If life were only like an old Bonanza *episode. Always a happy ending.*

I hear commotion coming from the hallway.

Now what?

Layla and Chenille come in. I notice Chenille has a catheter in her hand. She snaps closed the curtain between Maggie and me.

"What are you doing?" I ask, poking my head through the curtain.

"None of your business." Chenille yanks the curtain closed again.

"Layla!" I yell.

Layla pokes her head over to my side.

"Jessie, we need a urine sample from Maggie. We have to insert a catheter. That's all."

I poke my head through the curtain again. Layla has Maggie's arms pinned down, and Chenille has forcibly spread Maggie's legs apart and is trying to insert the tube into her urethra.

Maggie's face is contorted into a grimace and tears run down her face.

"She keeps closing up on me," Chenille says. She forces Maggie's legs farther apart, and suddenly Maggie lets out a blood-curdling scream.

I can't take it anymore. I fling myself into the wheelchair and race to Maggie's bed.

"Layla, please," I beg. "Just put a bedpan under her!"

Layla looks at me, frowning. "She won't know what to do."

"Just get the bedpan and give me five minutes with her. Please, Layla."

Layla shakes her head but tells Chenille to get the bedpan.

"I think you're wasting our time," Layla says. But then she sighs.

Chenille returns with a bedpan. They put it under Maggie and start out the door.

"Five minutes," Layla says.

I put on the meanest face I can muster. "Maggie. Listen to me. I know you can understand me. You have to pee into that bedpan. Now."

Maggie looks up at me with tears still in her eyes.

I raise my voice. "If you don't pee, they are going to put that thing in your twat."

She looks hurt.

"Pee! Now!"

I sit back and watch her. She closes her eyes. And then I hear her urine hitting the bedpan.

Music to my ears.

I smooth her hair and wipe the tears from her cheeks. "Good, Maggie. Very good."

She smiles at me.

Layla comes in and removes the bedpan.

"Well," she says, smiling. "Good job, Maggie. And you, too, Jessie. Thank you. Maybe you should think about being a nurse if you get out of here."

Keyword "if."

***

I am on a long, white, deserted beach. The sun is going down over a turquoise sea. I see something in the distance, coming closer to me. It is the white stallion. When it gets to me, it stops and nuzzles me. I jump on his back. He snorts once and then takes off at a full gallop down the beach.

We are in the air. He has wings, big beautiful white wings. We fly along the coast. I see dolphins dancing in the waves beneath us. We fly over the mountains, over valleys filled with lush tropical vegetation. We are in the clouds. Me and my guardian angel horse.

CHAPTER TEN
An Unexpected Visitor

Layla knocks. "You have a visitor."

A visitor? I have not had a visitor the whole time I have been here, well, except for "Kitty and Cats." I roll my eyes at the thought.

I don't want any more visitors. I don't want anyone to see me like this. In this place. I don't want to see the looks of pity on my friends' faces.

"I told them I don't want any visitors."

"Well, you might want to rethink that," Layla says. "This one's pretty insistent."

"Who is it?"

"Says his name's John."

John? That was my daddy's name.

"But I don't know any John."

"He's come all the way from Atlanta to see you."

I sigh.

Oh what the hell.

Something to break up the monotony.

Plus, I have to admit, I am a bit curious.

"Oh, all right," I say. "Just give me a minute to freshen up."

Layla leaves, and I brush my hair a bit. I look in the mirror. My hair is stringy and dirty. I need a cut. My bangs are hanging over my eyes. I toss the mirror on the bed.

"Jessie?"

A tall, handsome stranger stands at my door. He has reddish blond hair, piercing blue eyes and a slim body.

"Yes?"

"I'm John."

"So I've heard. Do I know you?"

"Not really," he says. "But it's time you did. May I come in?"

I shrug.

Who is this guy? What does he want from me?

He comes in and looks around. He spots the white guitar on my bed.

"So, you're playing it," he says, smiling.

I look from him to the guitar and back to him.

"Do you like it?" he asks.

"You? You sent me this guitar?"

He shrugs. "I didn't know what kind you played. They told me at the music store this was top of the line."

My mouth drops open. "Who are you? Why would a complete stranger buy me a guitar worth thousands?"

He scoots the chair close to me, sits down

and looks directly into my eyes.

"I may be a complete stranger, but I am also your half brother."

I laugh. "What? That's impossible. I'm an only child."

He looks me squarely in the eyes.

"Actually, you're not."

"You're trying to tell me that I've had a brother, a half brother my whole life and never knew it. That my parents never told me about you. Bull. I don't believe it. It's impossible. Who the hell are you?"

"It's true," he says. He squishes his lips together and nods.

I have the same gesture.

"I have a letter for you that will explain everything," he continues.

I lie back on the bed. This is too much for me to comprehend. I look at him. Really look at him. I study his face. He looks a lot like me—same eyes, same nose, same gestures. A million questions tangle up my mind. I feel dizzy. Either Daddy or Mom must have had an affair. It seems more likely it would have been Mom. Maybe with "Uncle" Steve, who really wasn't a relative, just a friend of hers. I remember how she used to drag me to his bar while Daddy was working. And how she'd flirt with all the men at the Moose Club.

Did she pretend I was Daddy's daughter? Was Dad not my real father? Or was it Daddy who had the affair? And the other woman raised John?

I feel faint, like I am ready to pass out.

John looks worriedly at me. "Hey. What do you say we get out of here for a bit? Maybe we go grab some dinner. Unless you've already eaten." He gestures to my tray.

"Ha! See for yourself," I say, and lift the silver lid.

He stares at the plate as if it's something from outer space. "What *is* it? Is it *alive?*"

Funny guy.

"It's SPAM. Our daily bread."

"SPAM? I thought they outlawed that stuff years ago."

I laugh. "I know. There ought to be a law against it."

"Well, let's go get some real food then."

"Go? You mean you can get me outta here?"

"For a couple of hours, yeah. I already asked that nurse, uh, Layla. Tell me… Is that a woman or a man?"

"I laugh again. "Layla. He/she is a transvestite. With great fashion sense, I might add."

We both crack up.

He has my *laugh.*

Then I frown. "I can't go in my jammies, though."

"Mine!" Maggie yells.

John and I both look at her.

"I can wear one of your outfits, Maggie?"

She nods.

"Thank you, Maggie." I give her a quick peck on the cheek before wheeling over to the closet. I look inside and see all the beautiful clothes. I select the long blue paisley maxi. Not really my style, but it'll hide my black ortho boot and slipper.

"Can I borrow this one?" I ask her.

She smiles and nods.

"I'll wait in the hall," John says.

I slip on the dress. It's a little large. Probably would have fit perfectly a few months ago, but it will do. Better than my flannel pajamas.

I look in the mirror. I could use a little makeup. Actually, I could use *a lot*. As if she is reading my mind, Maggie yells again, "Mine!" She points to her lips.

"You have lipstick, Maggie?"

She points to her dresser. I wheel over and open the top drawer. Inside is a cornucopia of makeup. Everything from lipstick to false eyelashes.

"Wow. What a treasure chest you have here."

I choose a coral shade and apply it to my lips. I look at Maggie. "Better?"

She points to her cheeks.

"Blush?"

She nods.

I pick out a pinkish blush, swish some on and look at her for affirmation.

She points to her eyes.

"Mascara?"

She nods.

I apply the mascara and look in the mirror. Not bad for a ghoul. I look again at Maggie, and she smiles.

"Thank you." I give her a quick hug. "I'll bring you back some food."

John is waiting outside the door.

"Wow. You clean up pretty good." He grabs the back of my wheelchair.

We pass Layla in the hall.

"Have fun, Jessie," she says.

As we pass the nurses station, I see Mullet and Cueball. One of them whistles, and then I hear them yukking.

"Go get ch'u some, Red. You need the practice!"

I pretend not to hear them, but John has.

"Who are those idiots?"

"No one important," I say, not wanting to ruin the moment.

John wheels me into the parking lot and stops in front of a 1966 white Corvette convertible.

"Are you kidding me?" I laugh. "This is yours?"

"What? You don't like it?" he asks.

"Like it? I love it! It's beautiful!" I caress the side of the car.

"Okay, then. Let's get you in."

He manages to get me in the passenger

side. "So, where do you want to eat?" he asks.

I think about it. When I bought my house in East Nashville 18 years ago, the only restaurants in the neighborhood were a Burger King, a Taco Bell and a German place. But since then, East Nashville has become a place to see and be seen. Musicians moved in and started renovating the houses, then the yuppies came and then the young hipsters. Now there is a sushi place, a rib place, a quasi-Mexican place, a Thai place, a vegan place and numerous overpriced gourmet places. Oh, and five coffee shops where seven bucks might buy you a cup of joe and a bagel. *Maybe.*

"I'd love a steak," I say, my mouth already watering.

"That sounds great. My wife's a vegetarian, so I don't get to eat meat too often."

"There's a Longhorn, but it's a bit of a drive."

"Longhorn! I love that place. Steer me in the right direction. No pun intended."

I laugh. We have the same silly sense of humor.

***

The smell coming from the kitchen almost makes me drool. A waiter appears as soon as we sit down.

"Hello." He pours us ice water and hands us menus. "My name is Daniel, and I will be your server. "Our special tonight is the 16-ounce prime rib. It comes with salad and a baked potato."

"Done." I hand him back the menu. "Rare, please."

"I'll have the same," John says.

"Would you like any starters?" asks Daniel, scribbling in his notepad.

"What about the crab-stuffed mushrooms?" John asks.

I can only nod. The saliva has thickened in my mouth.

"And what do you think, Jessie? Soup?"

I nod again.

Daniel smiles. "I'll be right back with some hot rolls. Would you care for something to drink?"

John orders a white wine. I still cannot speak, so I smile and point to my water glass.

The rolls arrive with a cheddar beer soup. I am done with mine before John even picks up his spoon. The mushrooms are amazing. But then the steaks land in front of us.

They are so large, they overlap both sides of the plate. I look at it, and then at John, and we both laugh.

"My God, I could live on this a week at the nursing home."

It is a piece of art. Blood red with crispy

fat on the ends. The potato is as large as Ray-Ban's hand. It is loaded with chives, bacon bits, cheese and sour cream. I start to dig in.

"Wait. Photo op." John clicks off a picture of me with the steak and then turns the screen of his cellphone towards me.

I look about 12 years old, grinning from ear to ear.

We eat, hardly talking until I am full. My stomach has shrunk, so I can only get a third of the steak down. I haven't even touched the salad or potato.

"Can I get the rest to go?" I ask. "I can sneak it into the nursing home for Maggie."

"Why not?" John says.

Daniel wraps the leftovers for me, and I stuff it all into my purse.

John orders us coffee. The first *real* coffee I have had in months, since Kelly bought me the cappuccino a lifetime ago. It is intoxicating. I finally sit back and look at my half brother.

"So, tell me about yourself. You said you were married. Do you have any children?"

"Yes, I have a son, Adam, who is 16, and a daughter, Autumn, who is 13."

"What are they like?"

"Well, Adam is a musician, plays guitar, like his Aunt Jessie, and Autumn, who looks a lot like you, is into horses."

My God, I'm an aunt!

"Horses? Does she have one?"

"Yeah. We bought her one last year. We wanted to get her a pony but she wanted a *real* horse, so we got her a gorgeous stallion. Name's Buck. Pretty fitting, I might add. Except for with Autumn. She's the only one who can ride him."

A stallion?

"He's not white is he?"

"No, he's an Appaloosa."

"Tell me more."

John tells me about his job as an architect and his ranch outside of Atlanta. I drink in the details like a person who has been in the desert without water for months and has just come across an oasis.

The time flies by. John looks at his watch.

"Wow, we've been gone almost three hours," he says, signaling Daniel. "I better get you back before they don't let you back in."

"Yeah, we wouldn't want that to happen," I say, rolling my eyes.

He pays, leaves Daniel a generous tip, and gets me back into the Corvette.

I don't want it to end. I want to ask John to just forget about taking me back and to take me to his ranch instead. But of course, I don't.

"How long will you be in town?" I ask.

"I have to go back tomorrow. But I can come by and see you in the morning before I leave. Maybe you could write up a list of things you need, and I could run and pick them up for you before I go."

Top and only thing on the list would be a set of wings to fly me the hell outta there.

"That would be great."

"Okay then, ready to saddle up and ride?"

"Sho' thing, Hoss," I laugh. "Pedal to the medal, *hermano.*"

John gets on the highway.

"So, what can this baby do?"

John smiles.

The engine roars to life as he hits fourth. The V8 takes to the highway like a bee to honey. John flips a CD into the player.

Fogerty, CCR, Green River.

We are flying down I-65, my hair whipping behind me. I close my eyes and drink up the cool night air. I recall my dream. The white stallion. The same feeling. I am free, racing with the wind. I am in heaven.

Before I know it, we are pulling up into the Carnation House parking lot. A chill sweeps over me. I shudder and want to bolt. John helps me out of the car and wheels me in.

Mullet is sitting behind the front desk. He looks at the clock and smirks. "You're late."

I look at the clock. *Late by five minutes.*

"I'm gonna have to report this," he says. "Happens again, it'll be your last little outing."

"Look," says John. "It's only five lousy

minutes. Give me a break."

"Sorry, dude. Rules are rules."

Yeah, some rules. What about those against sexually abusing female patients?

"I'll just wheel her back to her room," says John, glaring at him.

"Sorry again, dude. No can do. Visiting hours are over."

Shit.

Why didn't I tell John about all the stuff going on here? I was too occupied with stuffing my face and hearing about the family I never knew I had. I decide to tell him everything tomorrow when he comes. Everything.

"I'll be okay," I tell John.

"Okay," he says.

I see the reluctance on his face.

"I'll see you tomorrow," he adds. "Don't forget to write down that list."

I smile.

John looks at me and gives me a hug.

"Oh," he says, "I almost forgot."

He reaches into his pocket, pulls out an envelope and hands it to me. Then he turns and walks out of the front door. I sit there staring, wanting to run after him. I hear the Corvette roar to life and almost cry.

"Welcome back to the real world, Red," Mullet says.

Without looking, I turn and wheel away, as fast as I can. Last thing I want is Mullet ruining everything. Again.

"What kinda list you writin' up, Red?" Mullet yells after me.

I don't answer. I wheel faster.

I get to my room. Maggie is watching the television, a western.

"You sure do like those cowboys." I give her a wink. I wheel over to her bed and pull out the doggie bag. I put a towel down like a bib and take out the food. Her eyes widen with excitement. I start to feed her. She eats it all, steak, potatoes and salad.

"Tha-th-thank-ew," she says.

I stroke her hair. Then I throw away the bag and change back into my PJs. I hang up Maggie's dress and climb into bed. I am exhausted and just want to sleep. But then I remember the envelope. I open it up.

> *My dearest Jessie,*
>
> *What I am about to tell you will come as quite a shock. I don't know where to begin, so let me just start at the beginning.*
>
> *My name is Liz, and I am your birth mother. My mother and father are your grandparents. When I was 16, I got pregnant.*
>
> *Things were a lot different back then. Mom and Dad were shocked and embarrassed. The idea of having a teenage daughter pregnant with an*

illegitimate child was shameful. Even though we were a step above white trash, mom was always trying to be upper class. She was so concerned what people would say. She wouldn't have it. Period.

The father wanted no part. He was captain of the football team. He and his parents took no responsibility, and he refused to marry me.

Mom and Dad wanted me to have an abortion, but I couldn't do it.

Mom had wanted another baby for so long. She had had five babies that she either miscarried or who were stillborn. So I made a deal with Mom and Dad. I would go to a home for unwed mothers, have the baby, and they would raise you as their own. I would never be able to see you or contact you. Although it broke my heart, I knew it would be in your best interest, and that's what was most important to me.

Mom told everyone she was pregnant. For the last six months of what would have been her pregnancy, she claimed she had to be on bed rest. So she never left the house.

After you were born, they bought me a bus ticket to California and gave me a couple grand to get my life started. When the bus stopped in Santa Fe, New Mexico, I got off. The beauty of the land was overwhelming. I decided it was where I wanted to live.

I found a room in a boarding house, a run down adobe, and a job at a Mexican restaurant. I saved some money and enrolled in art classes. I painted in my spare time, and, after awhile, began selling some paintings.

A few years later, I met a wonderful man. Bob and I got married. A year later, I gave birth to John. If you are reading this, you have already met him. We had a wonderful life until Bob passed a few years ago.

I have kept up with you via the internet. There were so many times I wanted to contact you, but out of guilt and my promise to Mom and Dad, I never did.

I have all your CDs and listen to them every day. You are an incredible talent.

We found out about the car accident, and now with Mom and Dad gone, I finally decided I needed to let you know the truth. I hope they are taking good care of you at the nursing home.

There are not enough apologies in the world to let you know how sorry I am for deserting you. I would do anything to have you in my life, but I understand if you never want to see me or have anything to do with me. I will never blame you if you cannot forgive me, but I pray that someday you will.

If I don't hear from you, I will understand. And I will always love you as I always have.

Your mother,
Liz

There are also 10 $100 bills tucked in the envelope.

I bring the letter to my breast. I can feel the love and the sadness coming through the paper.

CHAPTER ELEVEN
Night of the Living Dead

When they call smoke break, I wheel myself down to the lobby.

Ray-Ban is sitting at his untouched puzzle.

The Professor is in his chair, filling his pipe. He merely nods at me.

Sissy is up. She is in her pink robe, but it is unbelted and I can see a black teddy underneath.

"Sissy," I say. "You're awake!"

"Hi Jessie!"

"I see you have on a new nighty."

She flings open her robe to reveal the sheer fabric. Her breasts are evident.

"Joey bought it for me," she beams.

I wheel over and close her robe.

"Keep it under wraps, Sissy," I say.

She looks hurt.

"I know. I don't usually wear black, but it does have pretty pink ribbons."

I wheel over to Ray-Ban and hand him

$100. He looks up, eyebrows raising over his sunglasses.

"Get us all a carton of smokes and some food. Get The Professor some good pipe tobacco. And spend the rest on tickets."

"Okay, cool," he says, pocketing the bill.

Shanika comes in and unlocks the door. We file out, last as usual, go to our spot, and Ray-Ban disappears.

The woods look beautiful. There are still leaves on the trees, brilliant shades of red, yellow and orange. The air is crisp with a slight chill, and the sky cloudless.

"Smells good, doesn't it?" I say to The Professor as he lights me up.

He nods, drawing deep on his pipe.

"Everything all right?" I ask him.

He frowns and shakes his head.

"Just haven't been feeling all that well," he says.

He doesn't look so good, either, but who am I to talk?

I glance over at Sissy, who is smiling with her eyes closed. Then I see she is caressing her breasts. She lets out a little moan, and her hand goes to her crotch.

"Sissy!" I yell, breaking her reverie.

She looks up at me, a little embarrassed.

"Oh. Oops, sorry," she says.

What the hell is going on here? What are they giving now, Spanish Fly?

Ray-Ban returns, passes out our cigarettes

and calls Wooly. I call Blackie. The two wildcats come darting out of the woods and up the porch to us. Ray-Ban and I take out our soggy napkins and place the SPAM on the wooden floor. The cats sniff at it, look up at us and meow. Then they back away from the canned meat like it's some kind of poison, which it kind of is.

I look at Ray-Ban. "They won't eat it!"

"Can't blame 'em," he says.

He hands me the plastic Kwik Sak bag. Inside is some bread, peanut butter, cheese and bologna. "It's the closest stuff they had to food."

I pass the bag around, and we all make makeshift sandwiches. Then I break off some bologna, and the cats gobble it up. I stash the rest in my wheelchair.

Shanika comes out, and informs us that smoke break is over. I remember that John is coming and wheel back to my room, eager to fix myself up a bit. And write the list.

A list of all the things that are going on here.

I get back to my room, hand Maggie a peanut butter sandwich, which she devours, and then I see the note on my bed.

> *Jessie,*
> *Came by to see you. They told me you were at X-rays. Sorry I missed you.*
> *I'll be back next week.*
> *Love, John*

"No! No! No!" I scream.

X-rays?

I wheel down to the nurses station.

Mullet is sitting behind the desk, reading a porn magazine stuck inside a newspaper.

"You asshole! Why did you tell my brother I was at X-ray? I was just out on the porch for smoke break!"

Mullet looks up, the ever-present smirk on his face. "Hey, Red. Sorry 'bout that. These scheduling charts get messed up sometimes."

"You did it on purpose, you prick! I hate you! And you're going to pay for this, you fucking creep!"

Layla comes running over.

"Jessie! Calm down! What's going on?"

"My brother came to see me, and this creep told him I was at X-ray!"

Layla frowns and picks up a chart. "That's *next* week, Joey."

"Really? Oh man, I guess I looked at the chart wrong," says Mullet.

"He did it on purpose because I won't fuck him!" I scream.

"Jessie!" says Layla. "What in heaven's name has gotten into you?"

"She needs a tranquilizer. Calm her down," suggests Mullet.

"No! You will *not* turn me into a sex-starved zombie!" I scream.

By now, nurses and patients are all staring at me. I see a look of pity on their faces.

"Jessie, that's enough," warns Layla. "I'll wheel you back to your room. You need to lie down."

"No! Fuck you all!" I can feel all their eyes boring into my back as I wheel away.

I get back to my room and am just about to get into bed when I see Mullet, Cueball and Chenille enter my room. Chenille is holding a huge hypodermic needle.

"No! Get away from me!"

Mullet and Cueball hold me down while Chenille shoves the needle into my arm. Immediately I start to feel the effects. They toss me onto the bed like a rag doll and leave.

"Nighty night, Red," Mullet says. "I'll come back and check on you a little later."

I fall into a deep, coma-like sleep. I don't dream, I don't wake up.

***

I hear voices by my bedside. I open my eyes.

Mullet and Cueball are standing beside my bed, one on each side. I open my mouth to scream, but no sound escapes.

"Shoulda played nice, Red... We woulda bought you some pretty nighties. Now, You gonna pay the price for being a bitch. But you gonna like it." He looks over at Cueball, and they snicker together.

"Shoot ya to see who goes first," Mullet says to Cueball.

I watch them as they throw out rock, paper, scissors.

"Ha, sorry, dude, you get sloppy seconds," Mullet says.

I try to scream again, but still nothing comes out. I feel them pull down my pajama bottoms.

"I tell ya what, Donnie. You're lucky day. I'm kinda in the mood for some back door."

He roughly turns me over and climbs on top of me. He is breathing hard, and sweating. My face is buried in the pillow, but I can smell him. He reeks of alcohol and disinfectant. I think I am going to throw up.

"Okay, Red, get ready for the *big* time."

Suddenly I hear a window-shattering shriek.

Is it me?

I try to scream again.

Nothing.

Then I hear it again.

Maggie.

"Shit." Mullet, climbs off of me. He pulls my pajamas up and turns me on my back. I watch them pull up their scrub bottoms and bolt out the door.

A second later, Layla comes running into the room. She runs over to Maggie.

"Maggie! Are you all right? What's

wrong?"

Maggie's face is red and contorted. She points to the door, her finger shaking.

Layla helps her lie back down. She sits at the edge of the bed, patting her frail arm. "It's okay, Miss Maggie. You just had a bad dream is all."

I can see Maggie trying to talk. Her lips are moving but no sound comes out.

"Now, now. Calm down sweetie. Try to go back to sleep."

Layla looks over at me. I still cannot move or talk. I try to plead to her with my eyes, but she doesn't understand.

"You go back to sleep, too, Jessie girl. I'll see you in the morning."

I try to shake my head no, but she is already walking out the door. When she is out of sight, Mullet passes my doorway and gives me the finger.

I start to cry.

Maggie gets out of her bed, comes over to mine and touches my face. She wipes away the tears. I try to tell her, "thank you," with my eyes. She smiles.

She understands.

I lie there awake, but not able to move. A zombie.

CHAPTER TWELVE
My Girl

I feel someone shaking me. I almost jump out of my skin, thinking Mullet has returned. But to my utter delight, it is Mike.

"Whoa, girl. Easy there."

I look at him.

"I came to fetch you for PT." He flashes me a smile.

I can only look at him.

"What's the matter? Cat got your tongue?" He laughs at his joke. "Come on, chop chop!" He pats the seat of my wheel chair.

I try to sit up, but with much difficulty.

Mike tries to help me, but I am dead weight.

A worried look comes over his face. "What's going on with you, Jessie?"

I try to talk but only gibberish comes out.

Mike frowns, reaches into his pocket and pulls out a candy bar. He unwraps it and hands it to me. Or tries to. He takes my hand

and puts the candy bar in between my fingers. I hold the candy bar in my hand, looking at it like it is a piece of moon rock.

Mike watches me intently. The chocolate is starting to melt onto my fingers and down my arm.

"What the hell did they give you?" A frown line spreads across his brow.

I try to answer. More baby talk.

"Shit," He shakes his head. "I'll be right back."

He rushes out the door and returns a second later with another man.

"Jessie, this is Dr. Douglas."

The handsome blond doctor leans over me

"Jessie, can you hear me?" he asks.

I baby talk to him.

He takes the candy bar from me and tosses it into the trash. Mike gets a washrag and cleans my hand. Dr. Douglas pulls out a pen light and aims it into my eyes.

"Her pupils are pinpoints," he says. "How long has she been like this?"

Mike shrugs. "She was fine a few days ago."

The good doctor opens my chart and scans it. "They gave her Thorazine last night. Says she was flipping out, cursing and screaming at the orderlies and nurses, hysterical."

"That's not like her. Something must have

made her go crazy like that," Mike says.

"Looks like they easily could have overdosed her. She's already on 600 milligrams of morphine a day. Jesus, what were they thinking? Way, way, way too much with the Thorazine."

"They could have killed her," Mike says with a disgusted look on his face.

"Easily," says the doctor. "I'm going to get her started on some fluids. You mind staying with her 'til she comes around?"

"Not at all," Mike says.

When the doctor leaves, Mike pulls a chair next to my bed. The worried look still stretches across his face.

"Well jeez, if you wanted to play hooky from PT today you could have just asked. You really didn't have to go to this extreme," he teases.

I smile. I *think* I smile anyway.

Mike leans over and softly brushes my hair from my face. "Pretty, pretty, Jessie girl. What got you so riled up last night?" he asks, more to himself than to me. "So riled up they gave you enough shit to kill an elephant."

I stare into his beautiful eyes.

Dr. Douglas returns with a nurse, and she connects an IV to my hand.

"She'll be okay in a while," he says to Mike. "Nice to meet you, Jessie." He smiles at me.

"Shank ew," I garble.

The doctor and nurse leave, and Mike sits in the chair, watching me.

He is so handsome. He smiles at me and then takes my hand in his. It feels so good, so comforting. I never want him to let go.

***

I am on a stretcher, attached to an IV, in a room where a few male and female nurses and orderlies are gathered. They are ignoring me, but I can hear them talking.

"That one over there? She still breathing?" asks a nurse.

"I don't know what's taking her so damn long," says another.

"Well, I can't wait any longer," says the first nurse. She is a short blonde woman in her early 30s with wire rim glasses and bad skin.

She gets up and goes to a cabinet. She grabs something from inside and walks over to me. It is a bottle of Clorox.

"I've always wanted to see what this would do if it were injected into an IV."

"Should probably hurry her along anyway," says the other nurse.

I watch in horror as she removes a long syringe from her pocket and fills it with the Clorox. The she starts to inject it into the IV bag.

They are going to kill me, and there is nothing I

can do about it.

I hear a car approaching from a distance. It comes to a screeching halt, and Mike comes running in.

"What the hell are you doing?" he yells. He knocks the syringe from the nurse's hand, undoes the IV, picks me up and carries me to his car.

I am sobbing.

He holds me in his arms, tightly. "It's okay. I got you now. I got you now, Jessie girl."

"Mike, oh Mike, Mike…" I sob.

***

Someone is shaking me.

"Jessie, wake up. It's okay. I got you, now."

I open my eyes. Mike is on the edge of my bed, holding me.

"Mike?"

"I'm right here."

"Am I dreaming?"

He smiles that safe, beautiful smile. "You were. Although, it sounded more like a nightmare. You were talking in your sleep."

"What was I saying?" As soon as I ask, I start to remember.

Mike. I was calling his name.

He seems to blush a little, and I know I am right.

Oh jeez, what a doofus I am.

I blush.

I shudder as the nightmare returns to me.

"You saved me," I whisper.

"Well that's what I'm here for." He smiles.

I *love* that smile. He reminds me of Dr. McDreamy from *Grey's Anatomy*, but with a taste of Tommy Lee Jones from the early days—a little hardness around the edges.

He brings me back to reality. Or the closest thing I know to it at the moment. He is patting my arm and asking me something.

"Huh? What?"

I was just asking how you were feeling now. Better?"

I smile. "Yes, much better. What happened to me?"

"You were given a shot of Thorazine last night. It was enough to kill you. When I came in today to take you to PT and saw how out of it you were, I called in Dr. Douglas, and he gave you some fluids to help bring you around."

"You *did* save me."

Mike takes my hand in his, and I stare at our hands entwined. They look so complete together. Like two separate entities that have now become one.

He waves his other hand in front of my eyes to bring me back around. "Jessie?"

I tear my eyes away from our hands to

look at his beautiful face.

I could swim forever in those eyes. I could kiss every crevice and frown line on his face.

"Hello? Anyone home?" he teases.

I look at him and chuckle. "I'm here," I say, embarrassed.

"Jessie, this is important. Do you remember anything that happened last night leading up to you flipping out? Before they gave you the shot? Anything after that?"

I think hard. Close my eyes. Bits and fragments of memories start flooding back like a great wave crashing over me. I feel myself tumbling underwater, trying to get to the surface.

Man. I am still whacked out.

But then I remember with the clearness of a summer day. I remember John was here, and they didn't let me see him. I remember cursing at the nurses station. I remember Chenille and Mullet giving me a shot.

Then *it* hits me. Mullet and Cueball had almost raped me.

What made them stop? Maggie.

I look up at Mike. He sees the panic in my eyes. I start to cry.

"Jessie, I want you to tell me everything you remember."

"I can't." I say not meeting his eyes.

"Why not?"

"You wouldn't believe me."

"Try me."

I shake me head. "I can't. They'll kill me."

He leans close to me. "Jessie, I have to tell you something. But it has to be our secret, for now."

I look at him quizzically.

He takes a gold badge out of his pocket, palms it and shows it to me.

I stare at it.

"Jessie, I'm a cop." He re-pockets the badge. "Undercover."

I look at him in amazement. "A cop?"

He puts his index finger to his lips. "I've also got a degree in physical therapy. That's why they put me in charge of this sting.

"Sting?"

"I've been investigating the goings on here."

"So you know."

He nods. "I know some, but I need to hear it from you."

"Wow."

Mike looks around. "I'm going to wheel you down to PT. No one is in there right now, so you can talk to me without fear of anyone overhearing, or coming in. Besides you *are* scheduled for PT so it won't look at all suspicious. Is that okay, Jessie? Will you help me?"

"Well, seeing as you just saved my life, I guess I could help you," I say, trying my best at a tease.

It works. He smiles. He helps me into my

chair and starts to wheel me out of the room.

"Wait." I wheel over to Maggie. She is sleeping, but I kiss her forehead and whisper, "thank you" to her.

We start down the hall to the elevators. As we pass the nurses station, I don't see Mullet or Cueball. Only Layla.

"You feeling better, Jessie?" she asks, looking up.

I put on a shit-eating grin. "Oh yes, Layla. Thank you."

"Well have fun at PT," she says.

"Physical torture," I say.

We get to the PT room. No one is there.

"Well, let's get you on the mat for some stretches and leg exercises." Mike winks and wheels me over to the mattress.

When he has me on the mat, he starts to lift a leg. "Okay, Jessie. You have to tell me everything. Start at the beginning. Don't leave anything out, no matter how unimportant it may seem."

"I can't believe you're a cop," I say.

"Fifteen years on the force." He smiles proudly. "Jessie, I am going to record this if that's okay with you."

"Sure, Mike."

He reaches into another pocket, pulls out a mini recorder, looks around and turns it on. He starts to talk into the recorder. "Date: October 4. Time: 2 p.m. This is Detective Michael O'Heaphy. Subject interviewed is

Miss Jessie…"

He grabs for my ID bracelet.

"James," I say.

He raises an eyebrow. "Really?"

I nod.

"Miss Jessie James," he repeats into the recorder, stifling a chuckle.

I tell everything. The thieving nurses, the bad food, the bedpan incident, the threats, the night I overheard the nurses talking about how much money they made by switching the meds, the blue food coloring, the threats from Morphine Drip. How she said Kelly's death was my fault. Then I talk about Sissy and what Mullet and Cueball are doing to her. About the lingerie they bought her and how they've been drugging her. And then, I tell Mike about what Mullet and Cueball almost did to me. Mike doesn't interrupt me. He listens intently.

When I am done, he switches off the recorder and pockets it. He looks down at me. I am crying, and he brushes a tear from my cheek.

"I am so sorry you had to go through all this. It is unbelievable. But you have been very, very brave. I can't believe how strong you have been, Jessie. But now I need you to be even stronger. I need you to be a good actress. You can't go off again. You have to be very careful."

I nod.

"Promise me, Jessie," he pleads. "This will all be over by tomorrow. I need you to get through the night. Stay in your room, or better yet, the lounge. Close to Ray-Ban. Will you do that for me?"

I smile at him. "I'll be okay, Mike. Don't worry."

"Good. That's my girl."

Another physical therapist wheels in an elderly male patient.

"Fuck, shit, piss!"

Toenail.

I let out a belly laugh and feel a huge weight being lifted from my shoulders.

"Couldn't have said it better," Mike quips quietly to me. Then louder, he says, "Okay, Jessie, time's up. You did really good today."

"What? No back rub?"

He ruffles my hair and helps me into the chair. "I'm gonna have to owe you a rain check on that. I got a lot of work to do, Jessie girl."

He wheels me back to my room, and tucks me into my bed. Then to my amazement he leans over and kisses me on the forehead. A quick peck, but a kiss nonetheless.

"Be strong for me," he says and starts to walk out the door. But then he stops and looks over at Maggie, who has been watching us the whole time.

"Thank you for helping my girl, Maggie,"

he says to her with a wink. Then he is gone.

My girl? That's the second time he said that.

I lie there, eyes closed, daydreaming about him. I feel like I am 13, and my first crush has just kissed me. I feel giddy. Nothing else matters. I am floating.

I look over at Maggie. She is smiling at me with an eyebrow raised. Then she points to the TV. *Bonanza* is on. I start to watch it. Little Joe is in trouble again, and Ben and the boys are off to save the day, riding hard on their beautiful stallions.

CHAPTER THIRTEEN
Head First

After a not-so-delightful dinner of SPAM parmigiana, overcooked pasta, and a brown salad, I wheel down to the lounge. It is empty except for Ray-Ban, who I am happy to see is almost finished with his Mexican beach scene puzzle.

"Hey, Ray."

"Jessie."

"Wow, you're almost finished."

He looks at me, frowning. "I'm stumped."

I see there are still quite a few blue pieces he hasn't put in yet.

He looks over at me. "Wanna help?"

I am stunned, but smile. "You sure?" I ask.

"Yeah, I been sittin' here hours and haven't gotten one piece."

I look at the puzzle pieces, pick up a few, and try them in various places.

No luck.

"Maybe if we try to connect them

together, outside the puzzle, we could figure it out," I suggest.

He nods. "Good idea."

Together we are able to connect quite a few blues. Then a few more. In no time at all, the puzzle is done.

Ray-Ban sits back, crosses his arms across his giant chest, looking smug.

"Cool," he says. Then he eyes me. "How did PT go today?" he asks.

I look at him warily. "Fine."

I wonder if he knows anything. Mike told me not to talk to *anyone* about anything, so I hold my tongue.

I look at the scene. It reminds me of a place called Zihuatanejo, a small town on the southern Pacific coast of Mexico, where I lived a few light years ago.

I had a little *casita* near the end of the beach. It was very rustic, but at night I could hear the sound of the waves. I had a great gig at a place called "Rick's," an ex-Pat and snowbird hangout, owned by a guy named, of course, Rick, and his beautiful, German wife, Heike. I played six nights a week and sometimes during the day when the cruise ships would come into dock for the afternoon, unloading hundreds of tourists.

Rick and I had a good scam worked out. When the bedraggled, hot and sweaty tourists would converge upon the "walking street" in front of the bar, I would get on stage and play "Margaritaville," and Rick would stand outside holding a frosty mug of beer, ice dripping down his arm and hand out a card that said, "Meet me at Rick's." The men would rush, in and let the wives do their souvenir shopping. After a while, the wives would return, dripping with sweat and eager to have a cold beer or margarita, too.

I made good tips; so did Rick. He had his own brand of tequila, also called "Rick's." He would bring me a shot on stage, and I would sip it and go on and on about how good it was. We sold a lot of those bottles. We had a good 10-year run.

The town sits on a beautiful bay, surrounded by mountains. At the town beach, a half block from Rick's was the *zocalo*, or plaza, and the fish market. Mexican fishing boats of all colors would line up under the palm trees.

As I look at the puzzle, so many memories of those glorious sun-kissed days come back to me. I vow right then and there that I will return one day. When or *if* I ever get out of here.

"Play me a game of pool?" says Ray, breaking me out of my reverie.

I shrug. "Okay, sure."

There is only one cue stick, and it is as bent as a 90-year-old woman with severe osteoporosis. The table is slanted, and there is a ball missing.

Ray-Ban is a bit better than me, but not by much. An hour later, we are still on the same game, when a tall, handsome, rugged redheaded, freckle-faced man walks into the lounge and over to us.

"Excuse me," he says. "Are you Jessie?"

I look at him. "Yeah," I answer.

He extends his hand, which I shake. It is hard and calloused.

"My name is Jimmy. Could I talk to you a minute?"

"I guess," I say, putting down the cue stick. "Excuse me, Ray." I wheel over to a far table.

The man follows me but doesn't sit down.

"I only have a few minutes," he begins. "I'm Kelly's husband."

The fireman!

"I've talked to our 'friend,' and he told me everything that happened before Kelly's accident."

I don't say anything, so he continues.

"Actually," he says in a hushed voice, "I don't think it *was* an accident. I had the car checked out pretty good, what was left of it. They did find that her brakes had been tampered with."

"Oh my God. I was afraid of that."

"We have a couple of suspects. The cops are coming to question that woman who overheard you and Kelly talking."

Morphine Drip.

"They think she'll talk since they have a lot on her," he continues.

I look at him in amazement.

Jimmy looks around. "Anyway, I better go. I just wanted to let you know what's going on and to thank you personally for helping us."

"I'm so sorry, Jimmy," I say, tearing up. "Kelly was a very special person."

"Yes, she was," he starts to leave, but turns back. "Thanks again."

I wheel back to Ray-Ban, expecting him to ask me about Jimmy, but he doesn't.

"Wanna finish the game?" he asks.

I am tired and emotionally upset, but am not in any hurry to go back to my room.

"Let's start a new one. You break."

We play a new game, and soon my mood lightens a bit. I am getting better, ready to put the eight ball in—actually the one ball, since the eight ball is missing—when Mullet enters the lounge.

I am so engrossed in getting my shot, I do not see him until he is beside the pool table.

"What up? I've got some balls you can play with, Red."

I miss the shot.

"You guys havin' a little thing goin' on? Guess you only like the dark chocolate, huh, Red?"

Before I know it, Ray-Ban kicks him in

the shins. Mullet yells and falls, grasping his leg.

"Motherfuckin' nigger!"

Ray-Ban kicks him again, this time in the groin, and Mullet rolls over, holding his crotch in his hand.

"I'm gonna kill you, you fuck!" He gets up.

At that instant, Layla comes rushing into the lounge. "What the hell is going on?"

"Fuckin' nigger is outta his mind! He attacked me for no reason!" screams Mullet, still holding his crotch.

"Watch that language, Joey!" scolds Layla. "I don't see how Ray could attack you. He's in a wheelchair, for heaven's sake! And even if he did, I bet you had it comin'."

"I didn't do nothin'," whines Mullet.

"No, you're just a sweet young man, right? I think you better sign out for the night."

"I'm on 'til three," he argues.

"Not any more," Layla says. "Go home. Now!"

Thank God.

We watch him limp out of the room, throwing us the finger when Layla turns towards us.

"Thanks, Layla," I say. "Ray-Ban was just sticking up for me."

"I know," she says. "I never did like that boy. He is just big trouble."

I nod in agreement.

I look over at Ray-Ban, who is still shooting pool, like nothing's happened.

"It's almost lights out, kids," she says, looking at her watch. "Y'all need to finish up and go back to your rooms."

"Okay, no problem," I say.

She turns and starts to walk out. I realize I am truly exhausted. Maybe I will be able to sleep well knowing Mullet is gone for the night.

"Layla?" I call after her. "Can you make sure he really does leave?"

"Yes, Jessie. I will be at the front desk all night."

Ray-Ban gets the one ball in and puts down the stick.

"Thanks, Ray," I say to him.

He shrugs his huge shoulders and smiles. "Been wantin' to do that for a long time."

When I get back to my room, Maggie is sleeping soundly.

The thieving nurse comes in with the fake pill. I pretend to take it, but spit it out as soon as she leaves.

Evidence for Mike.

The blue food coloring is already coming off. I wrap it gently in a tissue and hide it in the pocket of my robe.

***

I am swimming in the beautiful bay, gently slipping over the waves.

I see a monstrous wave rising in the distance. I watch in horror as it comes closer, getting bigger and bigger. I look at the shore. I am too far out to make it in before the wave hits me. I look back at the wave. It is on top of me and starring to curl. There is no going over it. I take a deep breath and dive into it.

Head first.

CHAPTER FOURTEEN
Shit Hits the Fan

"Breakfast!" Shanika whirls into the room in her usual fashion, dressed in blue scrubs with red peace signs on them. And red ribbons.

She delivers my tray, and I open the silver lid. Bacon! Soggy as shit, but bacon nevertheless. Blackie will be happy.

I make peanut butter sandwiches for Maggie and me, gulp down my Boost and wheel down to the lounge. Ray-Ban, The Professor, and Sissy are in their usual spots. Everyone looks glum, and nobody mutters more then a "Hey."

When it's time for smoke break, we file out, bring up the rear as we always do, and Ray-Ban does his usual vanishing act. Sissy, The Professor and I sit in silence staring out at the woods.

When Ray-Ban returns, we call and feed Wooly and Blackie the bacon. But even the cats seem out of sorts.

"Something's coming," says The

Professor, looking at the sky.

"Storm brewin'," says Ray-Ban.

I feel it, too. The wind has picked up, and the air feels electrified. A huge thunderhead is coming at us fast. At that instant, a zigzag lightning bolt shoots across the sky. A second later, a loud clap of thunder crashes, making us all jump out of our seats.

Blackie, who has been giving herself a bath on my lap, jumps off, and she and Wooly dart back to the cover of the woods.

Layla appears at the door and orders us all inside. The sky opens up and rain starts falling in sheets. By the time we return to the covered part of the porch, we are all drenched.

Inside, I wheel myself to my room to get into dry pajamas.

Maggie is watching *Bonanza*, same re-run as yesterday, but she doesn't seem to mind.

I get into dry clothes and back into bed.

I listen to the storm. It is unrelenting. But in some weird way I find it soothing. It lulls me into a half-sleep.

***

It starts right before lunch. There is the usual commotion of carts rumbling down the halls. Then I hear the sirens. At first, I think maybe it is a tornado siren.

But then I hear more, getting closer.

I jump out of bed and wheel over to the window. Police cars are screaming into the parking lot. Officers jump out of the cars and rush into the nursing home as if a riot has broken out. Three or four news vans pull up. Reporters and cameramen swarm the place.

I wheel over to the door. Cops race down the hallways. Nurses and staff members scramble. Patients stand in their doorways, mouths agape, staring at the scene before them.

Maggie is beside me.

"It's happening, Maggie." I slip an arm around her waist.

Then I see Mike walking towards me.

"You okay, Jessie?" he asks.

"Yeah. Wow! I can't believe this shit is happening."

Mike looks down at me. "Well, it wouldn't be possible if not for your sleuthing."

I take out the fake pill wrapped in tissue and give it to him.

"Maybe this will help," I say.

He slips the pill into his pocket. "Thanks. Good work. They actually just confiscated a stash out of the nurses lounge, but this will help prove they were distributing them to the patients."

I smile.

"We also got a confession from your old roommate."

"Morphine Drip."

Mike laughs and shakes his head. "She spilled the beans on the whole operation."

"Operation?"

"Yeah. Turns out it's huge. They were smuggling out over $100,000 a month in narcotics. Not to mention all the pain they were inflicting on the patients."

"What about Mullet and Cueball?"

Mike laughs again. "You mean Joey and Donnie? We got them on a few counts. Big time. They were in on it, too. Plus, they had a prostitution ring going on."

"Sissy?"

He nods. "That's why they kept her tranquilized so heavily."

"My God." I sigh.

"And a few other patients, too. Some of them willing, most of them not. We did get a statement from Sissy. She told us she was having sex with them, although she called it 'fun time.' We have her presents as evidence. We found a few sex toys in her drawers."

Right then I spot Ray-Ban in his doorway.

Mullet and Cueball are being escorted down the hallway, handcuffed and swearing. As they pass Ray-Ban, he sticks his foot out and sends Mullet sprawling headfirst, screaming obscenities.

"Oops," I say with a smirk.

Then another string of curses comes from down the hall. "Fuck! Shit! Piss!" I look at

Mike and we both laugh.

Ray-Ban wheels over to us with a huge shit-eating grin on his face. He and Mike high five.

"Good work, Ray," Mike says.

I look from one to the other. "*You* were in on this, too?" I ask.

"Ray's the one responsible for the whole investigation," Mike says.

"Don't tell me *you're* a cop, too."

"Ray's been our informer," Mike explains.

"Hey, hey, watch that," Ray-Ban says. "That kinda talk get me whacked in my hood."

"Okay, our spy then," Mike says.

"Yeah, spy, I like that. Just call me Bond. Ray Bond."

We all laugh at the silly joke.

"I knew what was goin' on in here for some time, so I made some calls, " Ray-Ban explains. "At first they thought I was just some mental case, but I kept callin' and callin' 'til finally I got Mike interested. Not long after, he started goin' undercover here."

"Unfrigginbelievable." I shake my head.

And then I see the thieving nurse and a few others being led away in handcuffs. Behind them comes Morphine Drip, also in handcuffs. As she passes by, she snarls one last snarl at me, baring her teeth like a rabid coyote.

An officer walks up to us. "We found the

journal," he says to Mike. It was taped to a bottom of a drawer in her room."

"Good," Mike answers.

As the officer walks away, Ray-Ban looks at Mike. "Journal?"

Mike smiles. "Jessie did her part, writing down everything that was going on in a notebook."

"But then it disappeared," I add. "So, she *did* steal it. I knew it! And I think she knows who killed Kelly because she told me it was all *my* fault."

"I think she'll be doin' a lot more talking when she sees a life sentence facing her," Mike says.

And then I see Krystal Burger being led down the hall.

"Holy crap!" I say. "No pun intended, but Krystal Burger, too?'"

"Krystal Burger?" Mike says.

He and Ray-Ban laugh at the same time.

Now we are all cracking up. When we finally regain composure, I see Sissy in her doorway, eyes wide, body shaking.

"Excuse me, guys," I say and wheel down to her. She is trembling in her pink flannel pajamas and robe.

"Sissy."

She falls into my arms.

"It's okay now. You're going to be okay now. It's all over."

"They took my presents!"

"We'll get you some more presents, okay? Maybe a nice new cuddly pink robe with poodles on it."

"Really?" she asks, her eyes brimming with tears.

"Yes, really."

I lead her back to her bed and tuck her in.

"Thanks, Jessie." she says and closes her eyes.

I close her door a bit behind me and wheel back to the guys.

"So, what happens now?" I ask Mike.

"We've got some temp RNs coming in for a while."

"They'll definitely be closing us down now," I say.

"Let's not worry about that right now, okay?" says Mike. "Oh, almost forgot. I got a message from your brother."

"John? You talked to him?"

"Yes. He had called and reported Joey. Uh, I mean, Mullet. We talked for a while. I told him what was going down and that I was watching after you."

"Wow."

Mike looks at me and Ray-Ban. "I gotta go, you guys. Again, good work."

He and Ray-Ban knock fists, and then Mike tousles my hair a bit. "I'll see you tomorrow, Jessie."

"Thanks, Mike."

He turns and walks away, joining the

other officers.

"Well, I guess that's that," says Ray-Ban.

"Let's hope so," I say.

"Gotta go rest some," he says.

I nod. "Me, too."

I tuck Maggie in bed and then get in my own. I let out a sigh.

I fall asleep instantly. I don't dream. I sleep, a real, deep sleep, for the first time in a long time.

CHAPTER FIFTEEN
In Your Dreams

I make my way to the lounge. It is empty except for Ray-Ban sitting at the table, a brand new puzzle in front of him.

I wheel next to him. "Ray."

"Hey."

I look at the cover to his new puzzle. It is a mountain meadow of wildflowers, a kaleidoscope of color. A single white stallion stands in the center of the meadow. I would have fallen over if not for being in the wheelchair. I stare at the cover.

Wow. Talk about weird coincidences.

Ray-Ban organizes the different colors together in piles. Reds, yellows, greens, blues—every color of the rainbow, and then some.

"Wanna help?" he asks.

"Sure."

We start working on the border.

"So, lotsa changes, huh, Ray?"

He smirks a bit. "'Bout time."

Ray-Ban, a man of few words.

"You don't think Layla was in on it, do you?"

He shakes his huge bald head. "Nah. No way. She was suspicious from the start."

I nod. "Good."

I get the feeling Ray-Ban doesn't feel up for conversation—*not that he ever does*—so I shut up.

We continue working on the puzzle in silence, except, every once in a while, Ray-Ban laughs. "Krystal Burger," he mutters and shakes his head.

We sit there like that, both lost in our own worlds, until Shanika whirls in.

"We're on TV!" she yells, running over to the set. She changes it from the ever-present CNN to a local station.

"And today, just in," says the anchorwoman. "An ongoing undercover investigation has come to an end at the Carnation House nursing home in East Nashville."

The three of us stare at the TV.

"Turn it up," Ray-Ban says.

The anchorwoman continues. "A number of the staff members have been arrested for their part in a million-dollar drug and prostitution ring. Here's what it looked like this afternoon."

The scene switches to the parking lot and a reporter standing in the midst of the raid.

Police rush into the building around her.

The reporter starts. "I'm standing here at the Carnation House, a nursing facility in East Nashville where a huge bust is going down. Supposedly, a major drug ring has been discovered after a three-month investigation..."

The camera pans to the nursing home as she continues. We see Mullet being led out, still cursing. And Morphine Drip. Then Mike leaving the building. The reporter rushes to his side and shoves a microphone into his face.

"Detective O'Heaphy, can you tell us anything more about the investigation?"

Mike's handsome face fills the screen. "This is still an ongoing investigation. No further comments at this time."

Then the camera switches back to the anchorwoman.

"And now, news just in about the investigation... Two men, orderlies, have been charged with the murder of a Kelly Clarke, a former RN here at the nursing home. She was pronounced dead at the scene of an accident a few weeks ago. Her brakes failed, and she hit a tree head on, shortly after leaving work. She was on her way to talk to the Director of the Carnation House, Jack Doffslot, about her concerns regarding patients' complaints when the accident occurred. Doffslot is currently under investigation, but has not yet been charged with any crime. We will continue to keep you updated as the investigation continues."

When they break for commercial Shanika looks at us. "Guess I'm gonna be doin' double shifts for a while."

I continue to stare at the TV.

"Y'all want me to bring your dinner in here?" Shanika asks.

"Sure," Ray-Ban and I say together.

Shanika whirls out of the room, and Ray-Ban and I look at each other.

"Wow," I say.

"Yeah," he agrees.

"Far out."

"Really far out."

We go back to our puzzle, using the edge pieces to frame it up.

After a while, the lottery drawing comes on the TV, and Ray-Ban pulls out our tickets and sets them on the table.

I don't pay any attention to the lottery lady until she welcomes everyone to the National Lottery drawing and informs everyone the lottery is up to $200 million.

"Wow," I say, not looking up from the puzzle. "That's high."

She rolls the cage, and the first ball comes out. "First number is four!" I hear her say.

"Hey, we got that one." Ray-Ban says.

The cage rolls again. "Next number is 14."

"Hey, we got that one, too," says Ray-Ban, a bit more excited.

I look over at the TV and then at the ticket on the table.

The cage rolls again. "Next lucky number is 11."

I look at the ticket and then at Ray-Ban. "Ray, we got 11!"

"Shhhh," he says, eyes glued to the screen.

The cage rolls again. "Fourth lucky number is…22."

"Shit on a brick!" yells Ray-Ban. "We got that one, too."

"Oh my God, Ray! You're right!"

The lottery lady spins the cage. "Fifth number is…7."

"Holy fuck!" Rayban shouts.

I look at our ticket. I look at Ray-Ban. He has taken his sunglasses off and is scrunching his eyes.

"And the Powerball tonight is… Lucky number is 17.

"Fuck!" yells Ray, jumping out of his wheelchair with so much force the table goes over. The puzzle pieces scatter across the floor.

He grabs me, yanking me out of my wheelchair and starts whirling me around like a rag doll.

"We won! We won!" he yells, hugging me so hard I think he may re-break a rib.

The lottery lady says, "To repeat those numbers…"

Ray-Ban sits back down and picks up the ticket. I grab a pen and write the numbers down as she repeats them. Then the lottery lady wishes everyone good luck, and a commercial for Chevy comes on.

Our eyes finally meet. "We won. Even the Powerball," he says, looking at me with saucer eyes.

"How much was it up to?" I croak.

"Two-hundred million."

I feel lightheaded. "I can't believe this. I must be dreaming."

"We're rich," says Ray-Ban.

"Let's go tell the others," I say.

"Wait."

"What?"

"Let's make sure first. Check the paper."

He's right. Let's not tell them until we are absolutely sure.

"Okay, let's wait 'til smoke break tomorrow. We can check the numbers with the newspaper," I suggest.

Ray-Ban looks at me, a huge grin across his face.

"Two-hundred mil. What is that a piece?"

"I guess it depends on how many other people hit," I say. "But I still think we're all gonna be rich."

Ray-Ban is deep in thought. "Two-hundred million divided by five… That's like…"

"Forty million a piece," I answer.

"Shit." he says. He puts the table back up and stares at me.

"Ray, am I dreaming?"

He reaches over and pinches me.

"Holy fuckin' shit, Ray!"

We sit there in silence a few minutes. Then I look at him. He has put his sunglasses back on, but I swear I see a tear falling down his cheek.

"What are you going to do with all that money?" I ask him.

He thinks long and hard. "I don't know…maybe go to that beach town you were telling me about. Sit under a palm tree and drink Margaritas all day."

"That would get boring after a while."

He nods. "Yeah. You may be right. Maybe I'll go on a world cruise. Go see that castle in Scotland."

"Mmmnnn," I say, lost in my own reverie.

What will I do with the money? Travel? Buy a house on a beach somewhere? First thing, get out of this place.

Suddenly it hits me. I look at Ray-Ban. He is looking at me, too.

"Ray," I start.

He smiles slyly. "Are you thinking what I'm thinking?"

I can almost see the cartoon lightbulb above his head.

"May…be…"

"You tell me your idea first," he says.

"No you."

"Okay," I say, "Let's say it together."

And we do.

"Buy the Carnation House."

We laugh so hard, we almost fall out of our wheelchairs.

"It's crazy," he says.

"Is it?" I ask him. "We could redo the whole place, make it really nice for the patients. People that have no one to turn to, no health insurance, no family. They would get the best care and good food… We could all still have our own rooms here…

"We could all have our own *suites* here," he says.

"It would be a good thing to do with the money," I say.

Ray-Ban nods in agreement. "We could fix the place up real nice."

"Put in a pool," I say.

"And a new pool table!"

"And a Jacuzzi!"

"And a gym with exercise machines!" he says.

"And a garden!" I add.

"And a basketball court!"

"With fresh vegetables!"

"A snack bar!"

"A concert hall!" I say.

"A home theater!"

"Road trips!"

"New puzzles!"

Ray-Ban and I are cracking up so hard we hardly realize Shanika has come into the lounge with our dinner trays.

She looks at us, eyebrows raised. "What in tarnation has gotten into y'all?" she asks.

Ray-Ban and I try to stifle our laughter.

"And what happened to the puzzle? The dang pieces are lyin' all over the floor?"

"I guess just all the excitement of bein' on TV and all," I say.

She eyes us suspiciously while putting our trays down in front of us.

"Well, don't go getting' too excited. Got your dinner here."

She pours us some lemonade, shakes her head and whirls out of the room.

We open the silver lids. Stir-fried SPAM.

"Fire Bubba!" Ray-Ban and I say at the same time and proceed to crack up again.

"I am never eating anymore of this crap ever again," I vow.

"I second that."

"Second that emotion..." I sing.

I push the tray back and sip the lemonade.

"This is too much, Ray. I think I gotta go lie down."

"Yeah," he says, beads of sweat forming on his brow, "Me, too."

I start to wheel away from the table. I

look back. Ray-Ban is picking up the puzzle pieces and arranging them into their piles again. It makes my heart want to break.

"See ya at smoke break," I say, as casually as I can.

Ray-Ban looks up and nods just as casually.

I get back to the room, and Maggie looks like she is asleep, but as I get into bed, I see she is looking at me, her eyes questioning.

"Tomorrow Maggie," I say to her. "Tomorrow is gonna be a brand new beginning."

She smiles and closes her eyes.

At some point a new night nurse comes in with my meds.

She taps me gently on the shoulder to wake me. "I have your medication," she says in a soothing voice.

I take the blue pill from her and when I look at it, she smiles and says, "It's the real thing."

When I rub it a bit, the blue color stays on.

CHAPTER SIXTEEN
The Last of the Bologna

The sun fills my room with a soft golden glow. I lie there, thinking how warm and beautiful it is. Then I think of Mike. His eyes, his smile.

Did he actually *kiss* me on the forehead? What would it be like to *really* kiss him. Kiss those lips. Touch that face. Hold his hard body pressed close to me.

I close my eyes again. He is still there.

…And he is leaning into me, a determined, desperate look in his eyes. I grab him, just as desperately, by his black hair and kiss him hard and hungry. I am going to eat him alive…

"Breakfast!"

Damn Shanika. Damn Bubba's SPAM.

Shanika puts the tray down on my table and looks at me, concerned.

I must look pissed off.

"What's the matter with you?" she asks. "Get up on the wrong side of the bed?"

I sit up, reluctantly. The sweet dream is fading.

"Sorry," I mutter and open the silver lid, then put it back on, looking at her.

All of a sudden I don't know what's real and what's not. What has been a dream and what hasn't. My head is spinning.

"Shanika." I say. "Was I dreaming? Were the cops here?"

Shanika looks at me in amazement. "Girl, what is wrong with you? You gettin' that dang dementia thing startin' goin' on?"

I look at her like she is speaking Swahili.

"You tellin' me you don't remember? Girl, we had the *Squat* team here! We was on the TV! We watched it together!"

I lie back. I feel dazed. Lightheaded.

Shanika shakes her head at me. "Eat you somethin'," she says. "I'll come back later and check on you."

"Shanika, wait!" I call after her. "Were we watching the TV in the lounge, with Ray-Ban?"

"Yes, his Royal Black Highness was there, too." She turns and walks out, glancing back at me once.

So, it was all true. It was finally over.

I think back to the lounge and watching the news story on TV, seeing Mike being questioned by that reporter. Suddenly I sit up like a bolt of lightning has struck me.

The lottery drawing. Did we really win the lottery? That lady calling the numbers. Was it the same lady as the anchorwoman? They looked a lot alike.

My head swims. I lie back against my pillow.

Impossible.

Ray-Ban was asking for my help on his puzzle in my dream. And the chances of that happening were about as slim as winning the lottery.

Ha! Right. Get a grip, girl.

I open the silver lid. And put it back on. I make a sandwich for Maggie and me with the last of the bologna, saving a little for the cats.

"Say, Maggie, what about we get dressed up today?"

She looks at me with the sandwich poised in front of her mouth.

"My brother is coming, Remember John? What do you think?"

She smiles and nods.

I wheel over to the closet and open it. So many beautiful clothes she has. I flip through them and finally pull out a long white Nehru-collared gown. It is so beautiful in it's simplicity. I hold it in front of me. "Maggie, this is beautiful. Do you want to wear this?"

She smiles and nods enthusiastically.

I spot a pair of bellbottoms and a red peasant girl style blouse. Stuff I used to wear when I was a kid wanting to be a hippy, but was too young.

I help her into the gown, and put the hippy garb on myself. We stand together in front of the mirror. We look like we have just arrived via a time capsule from the '60s.

"Wow," I say, "We look good, huh, Maggie?"

She smiles and nods, but then looks at me and touches my face.

"Oh yes, makeup, right, Maggie?"

She smiles.

Maggie. Ever the model.

I get out her treasure chest of makeup, and we sit on my bed. I apply it to her face. When I think I am done, I hold the mirror up in front of her. She frowns and points to her eyelashes.

"Oh, shit, sorry, Maggie. Forgot the mascara."

I apply the mascara, fluff her hair out a bit and hold up the mirror again. She looks at herself, then at me, and pats my arm. Then she points to my face.

"Yeah, I know, I need some, too," I say and begin to make myself up. I make cat eyes and tease my hair. Then we stand in front of the mirror again.

Woodstock, here we come!

The loudspeaker comes on, and a new voice informs us that smoke break is about to begin in 15 minutes.

"What do ya think, Maggie?" I ask. "Wanna go have a smoke?"

Her face lights up like the Fourth of July.

"Come on then," I say.

To my surprise, she grabs the back of my wheelchair and starts pushing me out the door.

The patients are already piling up at the door to the porch when we enter the lounge. Maggie wheels me to the back of the room. Ray-Ban is at his spot at the table, Sissy is on the couch, and The Professor is in his chair, filling his pipe. Just like old times.

When The Professor sees Maggie, he puts down his pipe and stands up. "Miss Maggie. So good to see you out and about," he says. "And I must say, you are looking exceptionally beautiful."

"Why, thank you," says Maggie, beaming and blushing at the same time.

"Maggie! You look so beautiful!" says Sissy, jumping off of the couch. "Wow, and look at you, Jessie!"

A new young nurse enters the lounge and opens the porch door. The stampede begins. We wait and then, as usual, bring up the rear.

We go to our spot. I break out the bologna and call Blackie. She and Wooly come running. I give them the treat and pull out a few dollar bills. I start to hand them to Ray-Ban. He just looks at the money in my hand.

"Aren't you going to go get our tickets?" I ask.

He looks at me incredulously. "What?"

"You know, the tickets," I whisper.

"Good Lord, girl, how much money you *need?*"

Now I look at *him* incredulously.

Ray-Ban continues. "Shit, you tellin' me we need to keep *playing?* Dang girl, ain't $200 mil enough for a while?"

I sit there stunned.

It can't be.

Ray-Ban hands me a newspaper, folded to the page with the lottery drawings winning numbers from last night. Then he hands me a ticket, and a piece of paper with numbers on them. I stare at them. There in all it's black and white glory are the winning numbers coming back to me from my dream. And they all match.

"What's going on?" asks The Professor.

Ray-Ban leans into him. "This has to be our secret for a while," he whispers.

"Ooh, I love secrets!" gushes Sissy.

"What is it, Ray?" asks The Professor.

Ray-Ban smiles almost coquettishly. "We hit the lottery."

You could hear a pin drop, the stunned silence is so loud.

"You're kidding," The Professor says.

Ray-Ban smiles. "Nope, see for yourself."

He takes the newspaper and ticket from my

hand and gives them to The Professor.

The Professor looks at the papers intently, then back to Ray-Ban. He is speechless.

"We won the lottery?" Sissy says.

Ray-Ban holds his finger to his lips. "Secret. Remember, Sissy?"

Sissy puts her hand across her mouth. "Sorry," she says.

"My God," says The Professor.

"How much money did we win?" Sissy asks.

If no one else hits, $200 million, $40 mil piece."

The Professor looks like he is about to faint.

Sissy claps her hands wildly.

I look at Maggie. "Do you know what we're talking about, Maggie?"

She shrugs, and to all our amazement says, "We're rich."

We all laugh. The Professor has tears streaming down his face.

"My brother is coming today, you guys," I start. "If you want, I can ask him to take care of all this for us. He can collect the money for us and start us all bank accounts."

Everyone agrees.

"And," begins Ray-Ban, "Jessie and I have decided we want to buy the Carnation House."

To my surprise, no one says it's a crazy

idea.

"Tell them how we want to fix it up, Jessie," Ray-Ban says.

And so we do. And we tell them if they want to go in on it, fine. If not, that's fine, too.

"I'm in," The Professor says.

"Me, too," Sissy adds.

"Me three," says Maggie.

Then I see Sissy looking at Blackie washing herself on my lap.

"Can we keep the cats?" she asks.

"They can have their own cat house!'" exclaims Ray-Ban.

"I think that was the last of the bologna," I say. "For us and for the cats."

"And the last of the SPAM!" Sissy looks at Ray-Ban. "Can we get Marvin back?"

I wheel over and put my arm around her. "If he wants to come back," I say.

"Oh good!" She smiles, her eyes bluer than ever. "Thank you!" And she throws her arms around me.

She hugs me tightly and doesn't let go. I realize how utterly kind and beautiful she is, how the little things mean so much to her. Any other girl her age would want to buy a new car, clothes maybe a house on Maui. But not our Sissy. She wins the lottery and is content to have two wildcats and a plateful of Marvin's meatloaf.

CHAPTER SEVENTEEN
Unfrigginbelievable

After lunch—macaroni and cheese out of a box—Maggie and I are watching an old John Wayne western, when John walks in. He looks very dashing in his tweed jacket, jeans and cowboy boots.

"Hey," he says from the doorway. "Y'all decent?"

He comes in, gives me a hug and pulls up a chair. His smile turns downwards in a heartbeat. "Jessie, why didn't you tell me what was going on here?"

I look at him. "I was going to the next day when you came, but they told you I was at X-ray, and you left. I was just outside for smoke break. When I came in, I found your note. I was really upset, kinda flipped out. They gave me a shot of Thorazine and almost overdosed me."

He does the frown-nod thing. "I know. Mike told me. I'm so sorry. I wish I would have known."

"It's okay. Everything has worked out."

"So, I guess they're going to close this place down soon and sell it, huh?"

"Well, that's what I want to talk to you about."

He looks at me, one eyebrow cocked.

I pull out the lottery ticket and hand it to him.

"What's this?" he asks.

"Well, five of us here have been going in on a lottery ticket everyday."

He tilts his head a bit.

"Well, we finally hit."

"Say what?"

"We won. We hit the lottery."

"You're kidding."

I laugh. "Scout's honor."

"How many numbers did you hit?"

"Every one of 'em."

"Every one?"

"Even the Powerball."

He looks like he is about to choke. "No shit?"

"No shit."

He shakes his head and laughs. "You're sure?"

I hand him the newspaper. He looks at it and the ticket in disbelief. "Holy shit! This was up to $200 million!"

"I know."

"We want you to hold onto it and take

care of it for us, if you would."

"This is nuts!"

"Will you do it? We need bank accounts started in our names."

"Well, of course I'll do it." he says, still staring at the numbers.

"Oh, and one other thing," I begin. "We want to buy the Carnation House."

He looks at me in near shock. "What?"

"We want to all go in on it. Renovate it, big time, and keep it as a nursing home. A private nursing home for patients who don't have insurance or family."

Now he is looking at me, still stunned.

"And…we want you to help us with the plans, you being an architect and all. We'll pay you, of course."

"Well, of course, I'll help you. But are you sure this is what you want to do with the money?"

"We're sure."

He shakes his head in disbelief. "Well, let me go see what I can do about this ticket, and the bank accounts. Get the ball rolling. No pun intended."

"Cool," I say and lie back against my pillow.

"Unfrigginbelievable," I hear him mutter as he walks out the door.

I have to agree.

***

When I wake up, I see a pretty older woman sitting in the chair by my bed.

She smiles at me with tears in her eyes. "Jessie," she says, "I'm Liz. I'm your mother."

I smile, even though I am almost crying at the same time.

"'Bout time you got here," I say, teasing. I open my arms and she falls into them.

We stay that way for an eternity.

"So, I hear you're an artist," I say, trying to lighten the mood.

"I try. New Mexico is very inspiring."

I nod. "I bet it's beautiful."

"Jessie, I had to come. I hope that's all right. I needed you to know how much I want you to be part of my life. Please, let's not waste any more time. If, that is, you'll have me."

I hug her again. "I have a mother I never knew I had. Of course I want you in my life."

And so we talk. She tells me about her life, and I tell her about mine. There's no awkwardness. Instead there is a connection, as if we've known each other forever. Then I tell her about the big bust and then about us winning the lottery and our plans to buy the nursing home.

"But why buy this place when you could do whatever, go wherever you wanted with all that money?"

"Because, I don't want anyone to ever go through what we have gone through. Of course, we won't be able to help everyone, but it's a start."

Liz stares at me. "That's the most beautiful thing I have ever heard."

"I've put John in charge. He's gone right now, putting everything into motion."

"Maybe I could help you with grants."

"Yeah?"

"Sure, I think a lot of rich folk would want to help out such a noble cause."

"But we're already rich," I say.

"Well, you'll need to keep the money coming in."

We talk on and on, making notes about all the things we want to do. The time flies by.

Finally, John returns, arms full of delicious smelling bags and boxes.

"I brought dinner," he says. "Unless, you've already eaten."

"Yeah, right," I laugh.

"Hope you like Thai."

"Love it!"

I realize I'm famished. Again.

"Sorry," John says. "They were out of SPAM curry."

I cock my head and roll my eyes.

"So I settled on lobster stir fry, chicken satay, and beef in green curry. And spring rolls."

My mouth is watering. We dive in. It is

the best food I have ever eaten. But I am eager to know what he found out.

I ask him about the tickets, and he says if no one else hits, we will get all the money. He opened bank accounts in our names.

"What about the Carnation House?" I ask.

He looks at me and frown-nods. "The Carnation House has been bought."

"What? Oh no. We're too late," I say, my hopes and dreams vanishing.

"I made a cash offer of $1.5 mil, and they accepted," he says, smiling.

"What?"

"I put down a deposit. I figure you're good for it," he chuckles.

"We bought it?"

"I also started a corporate account in the bank. I didn't know what you wanted to name the nursing home, and you can always change it later..."

"What did you call it?"

"I thought maybe you'd like it to be called Kelly's House."

Kelly's House. How perfect. She will always be here with us.

"I love it."

"Good. Now, let's eat before this get's cold."

So we eat. Maggie even feeds herself, careful not to get a drop on her dress.

***

"Knock, knock." Mike says. He stands at the door, his tall frame barely fitting in it. "Oh, sorry, I didn't know you had company, Jessie. I can come back later."

I almost choke. "Mike! No, please come in. Meet my family."

My family. How nice that sounds.

"Glad to finally meet you," says John as they shake hands. "Thanks so much for filling me in on everything."

" My pleasure," Mike says.

"So, how's my girl doing today?" he asks.

My girl. I'm melting, that's how.

He leans in and plants a kiss on my cheek. I close my eyes and melt some more.

"I owe you something," he says, handing me a box.

I open it. Inside is an ice cream sundae. A little melted, just like me.

I'm eating, and laughing, and crying. All at the same time. Not easy. But in the first time in as long as I can remember, the tears that are falling from my face are tears of joy.

EPILOGUE
Kelly's House

The autumn glow has come and gone. The trees in the woods are bare, and there is a slight dusting of snow on the ground. Kelly's House has been decorated inside and out, top to bottom for Christmas. Outside, multi-colored lights line the porch and windows. A huge Santa and his reindeer light up the roof. Inside, there are more lights and a huge Christmas tree in the new lounge. It is decorated with ornaments that the patients have made in art class. On the top sits an angel with long auburn hair. Her gossamer wings spread open as if to cradle the patients in them.

The renovations are almost complete. We had four or five construction teams here, working nonstop since the money came in. All $200 million. No one else hit.

The basement now has a gym and a basketball court. The PT room has been revamped with new machines. It opens up into the indoor pool. We have plans for an outdoor one as well and a Jacuzzi. The pool is equipped with chairs that can lower bed-ridden patients into the warm water. They love it. Glass windows surround two sides of the spa area. There is a sauna, steam room and massage area, also. And tropical plants and flowers thrive in the steamy air.

We added more rooms to the main floor, each with a private bathroom, TV with cable, and private screened-in terraces. The dining room opens into an outdoor patio for dining al fresco, weather permitting. We have candlelit dinners once a week.

There is also a music room complete with every instrument from the accordion to the zither. Almost all the patients are learning to play something. Ray-Ban has started a hip-hop band and is quite the rapper. Sissy, it turns out, plays the piano like Mose Allison and sings jazz.

We converted the lounge into a home theater. We show different movies every night and have occasional concerts. Of course, there are also popcorn and soda machines.

The new lounge and game room includes a new pool table and cue sticks, closets and shelves filled with puzzles, chess and checkers, books and every board game imaginable.

We have a small chapel, as well, and host

a non-denominational service every Sunday. We also have an art room stocked with easels, paints, pastels, even a kiln. The art and pottery classes are always full.

Our "free store" is loaded with clothes, toiletries and miscellaneous items. There is also a snack bar where patients can get healthy sandwiches and salads and sometimes treats like ice cream. All free. We have nicotine patches and gum for those who are trying to quit smoking. Our gang gave it up.

On the third floor, "The Fab Five," as the new patients call us, have our space. Each has his or her own suite with a kitchenette, living area, bedroom, bathroom and a terrace. There are also two guest suites.

Outside, we have a greenhouse that is already full of thriving vegetables. Come spring, we will have an outside one, as well.

There is also a cat house for Wooly and Blackie and the kittens. Yes, they had a beautiful litter. All of them have been neutered and spayed and the kittens are all going to good homes.

We appointed Liz as head of administrations, John as executive director, Layla as director in residence, and Shanika as head nurse. We gave Layla a $5,000 gift certificate for "Hair World," and Shanika one for "Ribbon World." Both got huge pay raises.

The old director was convicted of

conspiracy to commit murder and is doing hard time at Leavenworth.

Marvin is back, and the patients are looking less and less like *Survivor* contestants everyday.

Sissy has not had an "episode" in some time, and is very happy helping the patients. She is also quite happy in a relationship with her new girlfriend. They spend weekends at the cabin they bought on Center Hill Lake, about an hour from here, where Ray-Ban keeps his brightly colored fishing boat. He did go to a Mexican beach town, but got bored after two weeks. Besides jamming with his band, coaching touch football, and teaching billiards, he also has turned out to have quite a green thumb and serves as head gardener. He hasn't picked up a jigsaw puzzle in months, nor is he using his wheelchair. He and Shanika have a "thing" going on. Although, neither has copped to it, we all know.

Maggie has improved 100 percent. She has had some "work" done and looks gorgeous. She has even gotten some modeling jobs, and has been on the covers of *AARP* and *Senior Living*. She and The Professor are engaged and will be married in the garden next spring.

Me? Well, I bought a beautiful adobe in Santa Fe, where I spend time with my mother. I have a tour coming up next spring with the Alleycats. Kitty got a solo deal. Oh and yeah, I have a boyfriend. His name is Mike, and he is head of the physical therapy department. We have a date. A big soiree. It's Bingo night at the nursing home.

THE END

ACKNOWLEDGEMENTS

Thanks to Dr. Tressler for saving my foot, Dr. Press for saving my jaw, Dr. Beisman for saving my face, Vanderbilt Hospital for saving my life, and all the kind nurses in the nursing home who helped save my sanity. Also, to Jennifer Chesak at Wandering in the Words Press for believing in this book, and to all my friends and family who broke me out of the nursing home. You know who you are. And I love you.

ABOUT THE AUTHOR

Josie Kuhn is an internationally acclaimed recording artist, singer, songwriter and guitarist. She has been called "One of the leading ladies of the Americana movement," and, by Jim Ridley, managing editor of the *Nashville Scene*, "One of the greatest unsung singer, songwriters of the last 20 years."

Her five CDs have received rave reviews and awards abroad including "Best Tex-Mex" for *Walks with Lions* (in Norway) and "One of the best albums of 2005" for *La Luna Loca* (in England). Josie has toured and shared the stage with Rick Danko (of The Band), Steve Earle, Emmylou Harris, the Mavericks, and many others.

She currently lives in East Nashville's Little Hollywood community. In 2007, she was in a horrific car accident in which she suffered a broken hip, neck, ribs, pelvis, jaw, cheekbones and a severely damaged foot. She spent months in nursing homes while recuperating. Her first novel, *The Carnation*

House, is a work of fiction, however, some of the events are based on a true story. Names and details have been changed to protect the innocent and not so innocent. As Josie puts it: "Nursing homes are not just for the elderly. Young people in need of rehabilitation often find themselves admitted, as well, when they are victims of accidents, suffer from mental illnesses or struggle with substance abuse issues. There are a lot of doctors and nurses in these facilities who genuinely care about their patients, but unfortunately, there are also a few bad eggs in the basket."

Check out Josie's music and lyrics at www.josiekuhn.net and her CDs at www.cdbaby.com.

11047496R00126

Made in the USA
San Bernardino, CA
04 May 2014